Victor Storey

by

A.R. Johnson

Victor Storey

ISBN: 9798504960326

Published by
Liberty River Industries, LLC.
5201 Nations Ford Road, Ste D
Charlotte, NC 28217
www.libertyriverind.com
(980) 292-1754

Chief Editor: Delisa Rodgers
Cover Designer: Delisa Rodgers

LIBERTY RIVER
INDUSTRIES, LLC

Victor Storey

ISBN: 9798504960326

Published by
Liberty River Industries, LLC.
5201 Nations Ford Road, Ste D
Charlotte, NC 28217
www.libertyriverind.com
(980) 292-1754

Chief Editor: Delisa Rodgers
Cover Designer: Delisa Rodgers

LIBERTY RIVER
INDUSTRIES, LLC

Victor Storey

by

A.R. Johnson

Dedication

You were my friend before I even knew You. You gave Your life for me before I was even born. You gave me this book to write. I can't express the words I have for You because it wouldn't do it justice, but I will try. Jesus, I want to thank You for blessing me with this gift to write this book for You. I can't imagine the potential lives that this book will impact. Although I'm just a vessel, I thank You for choosing me to be a part of this. In the end, this will bring glory to You and the Father. Thank You for encouraging me and guiding me through this. Thank You for Your finished work on the cross. You laid down Your life for me. You bridged the gap between my heavenly Father and me. It's because of You that I can come to Him without shame or guilt. Your selfless sacrifice is greatly appreciated. I dedicate Victor Storey to You, Jesus Christ, My Lord, my Savior, my Friend.

A. R. Johnson

Table of Contents

1.	The Old Man	1
2.	The Encounter	7
3.	Victoria	14
4.	The Cab Ride Home	21
5.	Research	31
6.	Persecution	39
7.	A Vision	45
8.	Clarity	54
9.	Distant Friends	63
10.	An Encounter at the Hospital	72
11.	The Funeral	82
12.	Allen's Encounter	95
13.	Another Trip to Hell	105
14.	A Difference in Beliefs	113
15.	Round Table Discussions	118
16.	The Attack	125
17.	Growth	131
18.	A Spiritual Encounter	137
19.	My Final Visit to Hell	143
20.	A Visit to Heaven	152
21.	Five Years Later	163

Acknowledgments

Never in my wildest imagination would I ever think that I would be an author of a genuine book. Although it had its challenging moments, the journey to get to this point was well worth it. None of this would have been possible without the support of my loving wife, Zaranda. Thank you so much for your patience and encouragement. You and our daughter, Neriah, are my "why." I do this for you. I hope I made you two proud. I love you both with all my heart.

I would like to extend my best regards to Nathan Wahl and Kevin Kringle. I'm eternally grateful to you both. Your encouraging push at the men's conference in 2017 to write is the reason I'm at this point in my life right now. You all told me I could do it, and I did. Nathan and Anna, thank you for taking time out of your busy schedules to read my manuscript.

Mama Jan Davis, you were the first one to read my manuscript. Thank you for your honest assessment. You made me feel as if I could really accomplish being an author. If only you knew how much I definitely needed your encouragement to complete this book.

I want to express my sincere thanks to Sharon. I have never seen someone so determined to see someone else succeed like you. Your positivity is so contagious. Never stop being the person God has made you to be.

This is a huge milestone in my career. I like to thank those who took the time to read my sample chapters. Your honest assessments will help me to improve as I move forward in my career. I took your critiques to heart. I hope you like the finished product, and I hope we can continue collaborating on new book projects in the near future.

CHAPTER 1

THE OLD MAN

****

What you are about to read is my story about several encounters with Jesus Christ. He didn't come to me as God did with Moses in a burning bush. He didn't approach me like He did Peter when He approached him in person. Jesus came to me using the only way He knew I would listen—in my dreams.

This is my story; it is up to you to believe it or not. My job is to share with you how Jesus delivered the gospel to me.

My name is Victor Storey, and this is my testimony of how I became a believer and later a follower through a series of visits from Jesus Christ in my dreams. Before Jesus appeared to me in my subconscious, I was just a regular person doing regular things. Nothing about my life would excite you one bit. I minded my own business, respected my elders, and lived by the golden rule: Do unto others as you would have them do unto you. As far as God was concerned, I didn't believe in Him.

I didn't believe in Jesus Christ, and the Holy Spirit simply freaked me out. I mean, what kind of God would send out His "Holy Ghost" to help His people? It didn't make sense to me at all.

I knew of some people who went to church, but I could honestly say that they were only "Sunday Christians." No one in my family was a Christ-follower that I knew of except for my great-grandmother, who had passed away long before I was born. From what they told me, she was on fire for Jesus and was dedicated to Him. She desperately tried to preach the good news to her family, but to no avail. Even my great-grandfather rejected the good news when she told him about it, and no one was more dedicated to her than he was.

My great-grandparents had been married over fifty years before my great-grandfather suddenly passed away. At the funeral, they told me that my great-grandmother completely lost it. She took his death so hard, not so much because he was no longer here, but because she claimed Jesus told her that he did not make it to heaven. *What kind of God would send a good person to hell?* I thought. That was another reason why I could not believe in Jesus. I always thought that hell was right here on earth. I mean, just look at all of the calamities that happen here. All the wars, the corrupt politicians, pollutions, countless sicknesses, and diseases; you name it, it's here. My question used to be, "Why would a loving God allow these catastrophes to run wild all over the earth He created?" It was plain and simple to me; God did NOT exist. Period.

No one could convince me that God existed. None of my friends believed in God, nor my parents, not even my girlfriend. Sometimes, my friends and I would get together and bring up random subjects to talk about to pass the time. We would talk about any subject. One night, we brought up the question of whether or not God really existed. We all burst into laughter, agreeing how ridiculous it was that people believed God existed. God was a fairytale, a myth, a phony to us. If God were real, why would He send Jesus to die for our sins? If He were so powerful, He could just snap His fingers and get rid of all the evil in this world. I had never opened a Bible in my entire life, yet I thought I knew everything about God, Jesus, and the Holy Spirit.

My dad told me that a year after my great-grandfather died, my great-grandmother fell gravely ill. She was in the hospital for several weeks. The entire family gathered around as she took her final breaths. My father told me she began to speak in a language no one could understand. Then, as soon as she finished speaking, she passed away. They said she had a wide, peaceful smile on her face after she died. To this day, no one has an explanation for that occurrence. The doctors said she went insane minutes before she died. I guess we will never know.

I wouldn't say I was an atheist, but I knew I was not a believer. I didn't believe in heaven or hell, either. I thought when you die, you just don't exist anymore.

***

I remember a time when I was having a debate with a believer in Christ. He was telling me about how God is real and that there was only one way to Heaven, which was through Jesus Christ. I mean, I wasn't too hard on him because he was a real nice guy, and we were having a respectful discussion. I just didn't agree with him. He asked if I was an atheist, and I told him I wasn't. I just simply did not believe in religion. He then asked if he could pray for me, and I refused. I thought it would be a waste of my time. We both shook hands and went our separate ways. Later that night, I remember thinking about our conversation. I believe he was the first "honest" Christian I had ever met. I don't remember him telling me what I was doing wrong and what I needed to do—you know— those finger pointers. He was testifying about what Jesus had done in *his* life.

Later that week, I was with my friends having one of our usual discussion sessions. I brought up the Christian man whom I had spoken to a few days before. They jokingly asked if he had condemned me to hell. I laughed and told them he hadn't yet but went on to say that he and I had a surprisingly good conversation. We didn't stay on him for too long, and then we changed the subject. That night, I had a terrible nightmare, one that I had never experienced in my life. I've had bad dreams before, but this was unlike any other. I was in a very dark place, so dark I couldn't see my hand in front of my face. I could feel the dark. I didn't have on any clothes, and I felt like I was standing in mud or a mud-like substance. The smell was so bad, I could almost taste it. It was like rotten eggs and decaying flesh. It was extremely hard to breathe there; I was laboring just to inhale enough oxygen.

I began to walk very slowly and stretched out my hands to feel for something solid. All of a sudden, I felt several long nails or claws lightly rake across my back! I turned around and swung my fists, but nothing was there.

"Who's there?" I remember asking. "Where am I?"

"Home!" a voice answered. It was loud and deep when it spoke and seemed to quake through my whole body. "Welcome home, Victor!"

At once, I saw a tiny light in the distance. It was far away but was actually heading towards me. It appeared to be red, orange, or yellow; I couldn't tell. All I knew was that it was coming right at me. I turned to get out of the way, but a pair of large hands reached out of the mud-like substance and grabbed my legs! Suddenly, my entire body was stricken with paralysis. All I could move were my eyes.

I could finally make out what the light was: it was a wall

of fire that was crawling as it drew near me. I was beginning to feel the heat from it, and it was intense. At that point, I was desperately trying to wake up from the dream. I had had enough of it. I squeezed my eyes shut, hoping to wake up, but it wasn't working. I was still there (trapped in that dream), and that wall of fire kept coming. Suddenly, it stopped and just vanished! I let out a sigh of relief; that was a close one! Just then, the wall of fire exploded out of nowhere and completely engulfed me! All I could see was fire all around me; I was being burned alive! I could feel the fire seeping into my bones! My own voice was deafening to my ears, and my throat burned raw as I screamed at the top of my lungs! The strange part was, I wasn't actually burning up, and my flesh was still intact! I was helplessly thinking, *this is NOT going to end ...*

Soon afterward, it felt like a bucket of ice-cold water hit me, and I was jolted awake. I looked around and realized I was in my bed, drenched in sweat. I jumped up, ran to the bathroom, and looked in the mirror to check for burns. Everything was okay. *It was only a dream*, I sighed.

Afterward, I felt exhausted and cold. As I climbed back into bed and under the covers, I noticed the time on my alarm clock. It was 10:15 pm. I rubbed my head nervously. The last time I looked at the clock before closing my eyes to sleep, it read 10:13 pm. *WHAT?* Had I only been asleep for two minutes? It felt like I was asleep the whole night ...

CHAPTER 2

THE ENCOUNTER

****

The next morning came, and while eating breakfast, I thought of the nightmare that was still fresh in my mind. It felt incredibly real. I could still smell the sulfur, and the heat was so intense. No human could survive that heat.

I finished my breakfast and headed off to work. Later, I met up with my friend, Johnny, for lunch. I've known him since middle school. Johnny was one of my best friends. I told him about my crazy dream the night before.

"Sounds like someone put some voodoo on you," he said. "You smell sulfur?"

I took a quick whiff of the air, and I did. "Yeah, it's faint, but I smell it," I replied.

At the time, I didn't know it was me. As we ate lunch, I

noticed an older woman looking at me from another table. It looked like she wanted to say something to me because she would look at me and then turn away. Finally, the older woman got up and approached me.

"Young man, I'm sorry for staring," she started, "you have such a good heart, but you keep it closed. You have such a smart mind, an open mind. Soon, you will be in a position where you will have to close your mind and open your heart to see the truth."

The old lady placed her hand on my shoulder, leaned in, and whispered with a warm smile, "You are so blessed to be visited by our King." She then paid for her lunch and left.

"Whoa, that was weird," Johnny marveled.

It was time for me to get back to work, so I went to the register to pay for lunch. The man at the register told us that our meals had already been paid for.

"Who paid for it?" I asked.

"The woman who was talking to you," the man replied.

"Weird *and* generous," Johnny commented.

The rest of the day, I pondered over what the older woman said to me. *What did she mean, "I was blessed to meet the King?"* I asked myself. I was just thankful she paid for my lunch. She was right about me having a smart mind and having a good heart, but the rest, I didn't know what to do with that at all.

***

I showered up and prepared myself for bed. I looked at my alarm clock and it indicated 10:00 pm. I was still a little shaken from the previous nightmare because it lasted far too long for me to be asleep for only two minutes. I hoped that I was going to have a normal dream tonight.

Soon, I was fast asleep. Immediately, I began dreaming and found myself in a room. It looked like the scene of an interrogation room, the kind you see in the cop movies when they're interrogating criminals. The room was dimly lit and had a table and two chairs facing the opposite direction. I walked over and sat in one of the chairs. Minutes later, a door flew open and this blinding light came in. I could hear a loud, rushing wind blowing in from the door opening. As I regained my focus, I could see a figure standing in the doorway. It looked like He was clothed in the light! I couldn't see His face because of the light. Nervously, I asked, "Who are You?"

The figure took a couple of steps into the room and bellowed, "I AM!"

Right after He said that I was jolted awake. I immediately looked at my alarm clock, and it was 6:00 am. The nightmare I had the night before had me gripped with fear. This current dream had me trembling as if I was in trouble with my father or something. I thought about the older woman who had said I was blessed to meet the King. *Did she put a spell on me? Who was that person in my dream clothed in the light? Was He the so-called King I was supposed to meet?* I felt like I was letting all of that nonsense get to me.

***

I went to work and then later met up with my friends.

"Vic, you really look bad," Johnny taunted. "Have you been getting any sleep?"

"Yes," I answered. "I've been sleeping well. Why do you ask?"

"Your eyes look tired and they're red! That old lady getting to you?"

"Absolutely not," I retorted. "I wasn't even thinking about her."

At that point, I was not going to bring up the second dream I had about the mysterious figure clothed in light. I decided to keep that to myself.

***

A few weeks had passed by without a weird dream, thankfully. I honestly had forgotten about them and had since moved on. I was on a date with my girlfriend, Stacy, having dinner at a restaurant. We had been together for over a year. As we were eating, I suddenly remembered the words, "I AM" that were said to me and decided to tell Stacy about it. I told her about the older woman and the man dressed in light. When I finished speaking, she laughed.

"That sounds so ridiculous," she teased.

"I know," I groaned. "Who calls themselves, I AM?"

"He is the Great I AM," pronounced a voice from

behind us.

I turned and saw a man looking at us.

"I'm sorry to eavesdrop, but you were talking so loudly that I couldn't help but hear your conversation."

"Who is the Great I AM?" I inquired.

"God," he replied.

"You must be a crazy Bible thumper," snapped Stacy.

"I'm just a believer of Christ," the man said calmly.

"What else did you hear?" I probed.

The man told me it was Jesus who I saw in my dream and that Jesus, God, and the Holy Spirit are one.

"So, you are telling me that Jesus was in my dreams?"

The man nodded.

"You must have thumped *your* head with that Bible," I joked.

The man laughed.

"What's so funny?" Stacy demanded. "Aren't Christians supposed to be serious all the time?"

The man laughed even louder. "I'm a Christian, not a robot," he answered. "Look, I was just informing your boyfriend who it was in his dream. I believe Jesus is trying to talk to him."

Then the man looked at me and said, "You should listen to Him," then he got up and left the restaurant.

Minutes later, I stopped the waiter to get the bill for our dinner.

"Your dinner has been paid for already," the waiter said.

"Who paid for it?" I asked.

"The gentleman who was talking to you," answered the waiter.

"Good!" whined Stacy. "He needed to pay for our dinner because he ruined it with all of that Bible-thumping Jesus talk!"

Later that night, as I was getting into bed, I thought about the two people who paid for my food. I realized that they also paid for the people I was eating dinner with, Stacy and Johnny. I later drifted off to sleep thinking about it. I dreamed I was in the same dimly lit room and was by myself once again. One thing I noticed about those particular dreams was that everything was crystal clear, almost like a high-definition TV but better.

I sat in the same seat as before. Suddenly, I was aware I was dreaming, and I knew what was coming next. "Come in, I AM," I said sarcastically. I was looking at the door waiting for Him to come in. Suddenly, the room brightened up.

"VICTOR!" called a booming voice.

I quickly turned around, and there He stood. I could see His face, but because of the light, I could not focus on what He looked like. "Are you Jesus?" I asked.

"I am," He replied.

"Don't You think it's kind of creepy to show up in my

dreams?" I complained. I was not afraid of Jesus now. I thought I was having a lucid dream. I was overconfident because I thought I had control over this dream.

Jesus spoke, "Why don't you believe in Me?"

"Because You do not exist," I replied. "There is no God; God is dead!"

Jesus sighed. "Oh, you of little faith," He responded. "Your tongue is sharp towards Me; silence be upon you."

I went to speak, and I couldn't. Jesus had silenced me! "You will remain muted until you read Luke 1:11-22, and you will be here again tomorrow night … Hopefully, with some respect! Be awakened!"

I woke up with a jolt. *Crazy dream*, I thought. I went to yawn and realized my mouth was closed shut. I tried to pry my mouth open but to no avail. I thought, *someone has definitely put a spell on me.*

I ran to the kitchen to get a straw. I placed it to my mouth to pry a hole open, but it didn't work. After I was done panicking, I remembered what Jesus told me to do. I had to read Luke 1:11-22. I did not own a Bible, and there was no way I was going outside with my mouth like that, so I logged onto my laptop and searched for Luke 1:11-22.

I read that the angel had shut Zachariah's mouth because of his unbelief. Now, I had to wait until I was asleep to meet Jesus again so He could open my mouth. My best bet was to stay in the house for the rest of the night.

CHAPTER 3

VICTORIA

****

The day seemed to drag on forever. I couldn't eat, I couldn't drink, and I had to sneeze through my nose! I was hungry and thirsty and very uncomfortable. You never know how much you need your mouth until the ability to use it is taken away.

I realized I was rude to this Jesus fellow. I was going to hear Him out and speak with some respect. Even though I still was not a believer, I was not raised to be disrespectful, even if He claimed to be the "Son of God." I could not wait to ask Jesus all the questions I had for Him.

The night finally came, and I eagerly jumped into my bed. I decided to watch some TV until I dozed off. Before I knew it, I was in that room again. I had fallen asleep, and I was dreaming. I still could not talk; I guess I had to wait for

Jesus to arrive. I began to hum a tune just to pass the time.

The door opened, and Jesus walked in. Instantly, the room illuminated.

"Hello, Victor," He greeted.

I nodded.

"You can speak now," Jesus permitted.

My mouth suddenly opened, and I was able to speak. "Thank You, Jesus!" I exclaimed, then quickly put my hands over my mouth. "I'm sorry; I didn't mean to say it like that!"

"Don't worry," Jesus responded with a chuckle. "The next time you say it, you will mean it."

I sat down at the table, and Jesus sat in the other chair. There I was, sitting at the table with the one people call The Son of Man. "So, why are You here?" I probed.

"I'm honoring your great-grandmother's request," Jesus revealed. "She asked Me to visit all family members who were open to hearing the gospel, personally. You are the only one who is open to hearing it."

"But I'm not a believer," I retorted.

"I said, hear the gospel, not if you are a believer," Jesus corrected. "Non-believers become believers when they hear the gospel and receive it."

"What is the gospel?" I inquired.

"It's the good news," Jesus explained. "I'll go more in-depth about that when the time is right."

"Why are You visiting me in my dreams?" I demanded.

"This was the only way you would listen to Me without the distractions," Jesus continued. "Your great-grandmother, Victoria, loved Me with all of her heart, mind, and soul. Before she came home to live in paradise, she asked Me to reach out to her family members about the gospel. She was the only believer in her generation. After she passed, no one would even listen to the gospel, let alone accept it. You are the only one since Victoria, who is open to hearing My gospel. You are the fourth-generation descendant since your great-grandmother who is open to hearing the gospel, Victor. Let that sink in for a while.

"Do you know how many of your relatives I have spoken to that said no since Victoria?"

I shook my head.

"Over 1,500 relatives," He revealed. "1,541 grandparents, uncles, aunts, and cousins of yours through four generations have rejected me."

That was a sobering moment for me to hear that.

"I saw your heart, Victor," Jesus went on. "It is a good heart; your mind is what keeps you clouded. You question and overthink things. I am here to give you the truth so that you can make an honest decision. The Father has given you free will; I am not here to make you receive the good news. It is your choice to receive it."

I leaned back in my chair and thought for a moment. *Is that what my great-grandmother was saying when they could not understand her right before she died?*

"Yes," Jesus affirmed. "She was on her deathbed, surrounded by family who had no desire to know Me. She knew if she prayed in English, they would dismiss it. So, she prayed in the Spirit."

"The Holy Spirit?" I questioned.

"She had the Holy Spirit in her, who allowed her to speak in different tongues," Jesus disclosed.

"Why does God let all of this bad stuff happen in the world?" I pressed.

Jesus sighed and then looked up. "Oh, faithless and ill-informed generations," He pondered. Then He looked back at me, "For He in heaven has given you free will like I just said, and you choose to do evil instead of good."

I had never thought of it that way.

"No one thinks of it that way," Jesus uncovered.

I was astonished; Jesus had just read my thought!

"I want you to get a Bible," Jesus commanded. "I want you to read Genesis 2:17 and Genesis 3:6-24. You will find a more definite answer to your question there."

After He said this to me, I was instantly awakened. The first thing I did was open my mouth. "Yes!!!!" I exclaimed. I jumped out of my bed and headed straight for the kitchen! I opened the fridge and grabbed my bottled water. I turned the bottle up and gulped sloppily. The cool water ran down my face and neck as I drank. I didn't care. Just to be able to drink some water was all I needed.

I grabbed another bottle and drank from it. That time, I was more civil with my drinking. After that, I took out a loaf of bread, removed several slices, and stuffed the bread in my mouth. I collapsed to the floor as I ate and drank my bread and water. I had not eaten since the night before yesterday. Afterward, I called in to my job to take the day off.

***

I went to the bookstore to purchase a Bible. I had never opened a Bible before; now, I was in the bookstore looking to buy one. There were so many versions of the Bible; I didn't know which one to choose. I saw a woman in the same aisle, so I decided to ask her.

"Excuse me," I interrupted. "Which is an excellent Christian Bible to buy?"

"An excellent Christian Bible?" she chuckled. "They are all excellent Christian Bibles, be more specific!"

The woman looked at me and smiled. "You're a new Christian, huh?"

"No, I'm not a new Christian. I don't believe in God."

The woman scowled, "Then why are you looking for a good Christian Bible then?"

"Because I just want to read it," I retorted.

The woman came over, looked, and searched with her fingers up and down and from side to side the books. "Ah, here it is," she blurted. "This is a King James Version. This one is most popular with Christians."

"Are you a Christian?" I inquired.

"I used to be," she snapped back.

"Why did you stop being a Christian?"

"Too many rules! You can't do this; you can't do that. I used to go to church, but I stopped going because the people at church would talk about each other more than help each other. They even talked about me."

"That's too bad; I'm sorry to hear that," I apologized.

I thanked the woman for helping me out, and then I went to the counter to pay for my Bible. When I got home, I began to go over the scriptures Jesus had instructed me to read. I began to see what God really wanted for us. He did not intend for us to live the way we all do now. I also read that Adam and Eve disobeyed God and that caused sin to enter the world.

Now I had more questions for Jesus. I started to think that maybe this Jesus guy was the real deal. He shut my mouth in my dream. Then my mouth was shut in real life. The scriptures He gave me in my dream turned out to be accurate in real life.

My heart began to close, and my mind took over. *What if this is some kind of witchcraft?* I thought. *Is someone practicing some dark magic on me?* I read stories about people practicing stuff like that.

Talking to that woman at the bookstore had also

reminded me about how churches could be. I heard the stories from the Sunday Christians about how the church looks down on "sinners" and act as if they had never done a wrong thing in their lives. I made a point to bring that up to Jesus at our next encounter.

CHAPTER 4

THE CAB RIDE HOME

****

Several days had gone by without a visit from Jesus. I was convinced that a spell was put on me. I was beginning to believe Jesus was a fraud because my heart had hardened towards Him. I did believe my great-grandmother was a Christian; however, I did question if she was with Jesus in paradise.

Johnny called and invited me to a private party at a local sports bar to have a few drinks. It had been a while since I had gone out, so I decided to go. The place was packed, and we could barely find seats.

"I love a good crowd," announced Johnny.

"Yeah, but this is too crowded for my liking," I murmured.

A man stood up on one of the chairs and shouted,

"UNTIL 10:30 PM, ALL OF THE DRINKS WILL BE ON ME!"

I looked at the clock on the wall, and it was only 9 pm. The crowd erupted in a great cheer.

"Jackpot," I sneered.

People raced to the bar to get in line for their free drinks. Johnny and I stayed back until the line got shorter.

"Word has it that guy received a huge inheritance from a distant relative that passed away," Johnny acknowledged. "He's moving to Los Angeles tomorrow."

"Sweet," I nodded.

After a while, I noticed the line at the bar was short, so Johnny and I got in line to get our free drinks.

"Two beers for me," I bellowed with confidence. The bartender gave us our drinks, and we went back to our table.

11:30 pm rolled around. Most of the crowd had gone, as were the free drinks most of the people showed up for. Johnny and I decided to call it a night. I called a cab, and we headed home. Johnny lived closer, so we headed to his place first to drop him off.

"Blessings to you," greeted the cab driver.

We both said hi, and then quietly looked at each other and laughed silently. Johnny told the cab driver his address first, and we were on our way.

"You guys enjoy the free drinks tonight?" pried the cab driver.

Johnny looked at me with bewilderment. "How did you

know our drinks were free?" he shot back.

"That's not important," returned the cab driver. "What's important is your salvation."

Johnny rolled his eyes and looked at me. "How do you keep attracting these weirdos?"

I shrugged.

"Why am I a weirdo because I asked about your salvation?" the driver questioned.

"Yes!" Johnny retaliated. "You are a Bible-thumping weirdo!"

"Calm down, Johnny," I interrupted. "Let the man talk! It's falling on deaf ears anyway!"

"If you were to die tonight, where would you go?" the cab driver continued.

"Nowhere, because heaven or hell doesn't exist!" shouted Johnny.

The driver looked at me. "How about you, young man?"

"I-I don't know," I said nervously.

"I'm gonna tell you young men something," started the cab driver. "Hell is a very real place. There is no rest; you will be hungry, and you will be thirsty, sad, and remorseful. There will be weeping and gnashing of teeth. You will have all of your memories and regrets, all while being tortured alive. But, by believing what Jesus Christ did for us, and turning away from your sins, you two can avoid that terrible place."

"Where is the proof of all of this?" demanded Johnny

angrily.

The driver pulled over, turned towards us, and removed his hat. He then pointed to a long, thick scar on the side of his head. With his fist, he slightly knocked on the side of his head. The sound it made was not normal.

"Metal plate," explained the driver. "I was robbed at gunpoint three years ago. After they took all of seven dollars, one of them shot me in the head. I was dead on the scene. I was a nonbeliever, so I went to hell."

Johnny folded his arms in disgust.

"The Bible describes this place, but I did not believe it until I was actually there. One of the paramedics decided to double-check for a pulse just to make sure. Thank God he did! He found a faint pulse. I could tell they were working on me because I was being tormented in hell one minute, and then it was total darkness the next. I'll tell you what, darkness never felt so good compared to hell. They finally brought me back to the living side, THANK YOU JESUS!

"I was in a coma for six months. The doctors told my family if I were to ever come out of my coma, I would have the mind of a five-year-old child. They were obviously wrong. The first thing I did when I woke up was give my life to Jesus Christ. The doctors also told my family that I could be a vegetable for the rest of my life, but Jesus told me while I was in my coma that I would make a full recovery, and I did. Now I'm here as living proof that Jesus is real, and hell is also real."

"Cool story, bro," snapped Johnny. "Look, what they did to you was not cool, and I'm glad you are alive, but that hell thing you're talking about was all in your mind. Science has proven that to be true."

The driver laughed and shook his head. "I never heard anyone who had a near-death experience say anything about science when they came back, you know why? Science does not exist when you're in hell!"

The driver turned around and started to drive again. When he arrived at Johnny's house, he told him to keep his money; the ride was on him.

"Thanks," grumbled Johnny. "I'll catch you later, Vic."

The driver looked at me through the rearview mirror. "Where to?" he asked.

I gave him my address, and he started to drive. After a few minutes, he spoke. "So, you're on the fence, huh?"

"How do you know I'm on the fence," I quipped. "Did Jesus tell you?"

"Nope," the driver confirmed. "I could see it on your face while I was talking. Your friend's heart is hardened almost beyond repair. It will take a lot for him to come around. He has to open his heart, but it's not too late for him. Nothing is impossible with God."

"My friend is fine," I hissed. "There is nothing wrong with him."

"Young man, Jesus loves you," the driver continued.

"He laid down His life so that you can live. Open up your heart and give Him a chance. We are all made in the image of God. That means we are made to live forever. Our bodies are temporary, but our spirits last for eternity. Where you spend that eternity depends on the decision you make while you are alive to make it. Accepting Jesus as your savior and repenting of your sins is the first step to eternal life."

"I really don't believe everything you are saying to me," I contended.

"Ask Him to guide you," the driver implored. "There is something in you that wants to know more about Him; I can sense it in you."

The driver dropped me off, free of charge. I thanked him, he nodded, and he drove off. As soon as I got inside my house, I sat in my recliner and watched TV. My mind was still on the driver who had shown us the gunshot wound to his head. *It's a shame how people can be so cruel to each other*, I thought. *How can someone look into someone else's eyes and pull the trigger with the intent to kill?* I had compassion for the driver, but my anger was rekindled towards Jesus. I wanted to know more about this hell place.

"Jesus," I started, "it's been a while since You showed Yourself to me. Where are You? I'm going to bed, and I expect You to be there when I start dreaming."

I began to laugh aloud. *Man, I sound crazy!* I got into bed, and soon I was fast asleep. Minutes later, I found myself in that dim room again. Jesus soon came in, and the room brightened up again.

"Victor, you have a lot on your mind. Tell me."

"Why are the people in Your church so mean to each other?" I interrogated. "Aren't they supposed to help the lost?"

Jesus paused. "If you sit in a garage, does that make you a car?"

"No," I answered.

"Then neither does going to church make you a follower of Mine," Jesus said. "Matthew 7:20 says by their fruits you will know them."

"What does that mean?" I questioned.

"It means if you are one of Mine, you will produce good things. If you are not, then you will produce bad things. Not everyone who goes to church is considered My people. Many of them don't even worship Me. Even some who hold high positions in the church."

Jesus put His head down as He spoke. "Yet, I still reach out to them to tell them to change their ways."

"Do they?" I inquired.

"Some of them do, but many of them ignore me and continue in their wicked ways in the church."

"Why doesn't the church kick them out?" I proposed.

"Would you kick a patient out of the hospital because they didn't get better?"

"No," I reckoned.

"I know who is really with Me, and I know who is not," Jesus shared. "If they don't turn away from their evil ways, they will perish. Over the years, My church has become diluted with the things of this world. To some, they see nothing wrong with this. They feel My church has become obsolete and needs to "catch up" with the times. My Father has not changed; He is the same yesterday, today, and forever, so why should the church change to accommodate the world?"

"I understand," I chimed in. "Was that driver telling the truth about going to hell?" I asked further.

"Kyle was telling the truth," Jesus affirmed.

"Kyle?"

"Yes, Kyle. I know all of My sheep by name," Jesus gleamed with a smile. "Kyle was not a bad person by the world's standards, but he was wicked in My eyes because he was living in sin just like you and your friends. Kyle died without repenting of his sins, so he went to that terrible place called hell. His life was spared; he repented and asked Me to be his savior. He is one of My faithful followers now."

I sighed and leaned back in my chair. "That is a lot to take in."

"Victor, you harden your heart towards Me because you do not know Me. I am not your enemy. However, there is an enemy who you and most of the world have been neglecting to recognize, and he is the main culprit behind why the world is the way it is today. Yet, people like to blame My Father for the evil He "allows" in the world."

"Who are you talking about? The devil?" I questioned.

"Yes," Jesus answered.

"I kind of like that character," I chortled.

"Satan hates you," Jesus rebutted. "His sole mission is to destroy you. Yet, he has his followers, and yet, he still hates them."

Jesus was shaking his head in disappointment as He was saying this to me. "Victor, I want you to read the Gospel of John. I want you to see how much I care about not just you, but everyone. I love you, Victor, and I don't want to see you perish. People are dying as we speak that rejected Me, and they will spend eternity in hell."

"How come you are here with me?" I wondered. "Shouldn't you be helping them instead of talking to me?"

"My child, I am with them; I am omnipresent. I'm with you, your friends, and every living soul on this planet," Jesus explained. "Read the Gospel of John with the intent to learn," Jesus instructed.

I did not want to read the Bible. Personally, I thought it was a boring book. Jesus knew my thoughts and spoke, "How can you be bored with a book you never read?"

"I guess you are right," I agreed. "I will give it an honest read."

"Victor, before I wake you up, I want to show you something."

Instantly I was transported to an all-white room. It was the whitest white that I have ever seen. I looked to speak to Jesus, but He wasn't there. Then a woman walked in and smiled at me. I didn't recognize her. She was young, probably about my age: 24 or 25 years old. She had beautiful long hair. Her garments shined so brightly that I had to squint to focus on her face.

"Victor!" she gleamed in excitement.

"Who are you?" I inquired. "Do I know you?"

"I'm your great-grandmother, Victoria!" she affirmed.

My jaw dropped. "How can this be?" I demanded. "You died before I was born!"

Victoria smiled. She walked towards me, and she hugged me. "My great-grandson, you have so much to learn. Read the book of John as Jesus said."

I suddenly woke up, hugging my pillow, still in shock about meeting my great-grandmother.

CHAPTER 5

RESEARCH

****

I went to my mother's house the next day. I wanted to see how my great-grandmother looked when she was younger just to get confirmation. If anyone had that picture, it would be my mom.

My mom and dad divorced while I was still a kid, but they maintained their friendship for my sake. Victoria was my dad's grandmother, but my mom keeps all the family pictures because she loves family history.

"Victor! It's so good to see you!"

"Hi Mom, I missed you!" I exclaimed.

"What brings you home?" she probed.

"I wanted to know if you had a picture of Grandma Victoria stored somewhere," I responded. "A younger picture of her; do you have one?"

A bewildered look came across my mother's face.

"We might have to take a trip to the attic," Mom stated. "Do you mind me asking why you want to see a younger picture of her?"

"I never saw a picture of her when she was young," I replied. "In every picture I was shown, she was old."

"I believe I saw a couple of pictures of her in the attic, let's go."

We went to the attic and started looking for Victoria's name on the boxes. My mom is a total neat freak. She had all of the boxes labeled with individual names on it. I had my name on a box, my dad had his name on a box, and I even saw a few distant cousins' names on boxes. It wasn't hard to find Victoria's box.

My mom dragged the box out and opened it. We sifted through her things. I saw her wedding ring, some of her clothes, a few pictures of my dad when he was a child, and an old diary. Finally, we saw an old yearbook from her college days. I opened the yearbook, and a picture fell out. I looked at it and saw Grandma Victoria! She looked exactly like who I saw in my dream!

"She was 22 years old in that picture," Mom explained.

"She's beautiful," I stuttered.

"Yes, she is," Mom agreed.

"Mom, do you believe in God?"

"Not really," she disclosed. "I believe more in evolution

than being created by an imaginary being people call "god." Why do you ask?"

I really wanted to tell her about my visits with Jesus, but then I remembered when He told me that my parents didn't believe.

"Just curious," I mentioned. "Can I take this picture home?"

"Sure, just make sure you bring it back in one piece," Mom demanded, pointing her finger at me.

"Ok, Mom." I hugged her and left to go back home. I had some reading to do.

***

I really didn't know what to expect, reading the book of John. I didn't know who he was or why I was reading about him. I figured I would just plow through the book and see what happens. One of the first things I began to notice as I read was how quickly I became locked into the book; so much for plowing through. I began to read how Jesus healed so many people. I never knew that Jesus was a healer. As I read on, I began to notice how kind He was to the people who followed Him. I could feel the compassion He had for the people He healed. The only Jesus I knew about before I read the Bible was the one that other people told me about, and I really did not like that description of Him.

Thanks to my great-grandmother's prayers many years ago, Jesus actually visited me in my dreams! I put the Bible down and reflected on that for a moment. Jesus is omnipresent, He's striking up a conversation with me in my subconscious mind, and He is still helping the world at the same time!

Excitedly, I began to read on. The Pharisees were the only people who Jesus really spoke to with anger. They tried to catch Him up to see if they could find something to accuse Him of, but His truthful words always prevailed. Here He was, the Son of God, and they didn't believe Him! They wanted Him to show them a sign. DUH! He was healing the sick and casting out demons! HE EVEN RAISED PEOPLE FROM THE DEAD! All of these good things Jesus did, and they still wanted to kill Him. The more I read, the more I understood that Jesus was not just a man; He really was the Son of God.

I was upset when they nailed Him to the cross, and He died. Although Jesus knew He was going to die, He still went through with it to save humanity from their sins. I could just feel the pain and anguish of His disciples. I was so angry with Judas for selling out Jesus like that, but I understood that it had to be done. When Jesus came back from the dead, I was so excited. Then I realized that this was the resurrection! This was Easter! It wasn't about bunny rabbits and colored eggs. It was about Jesus coming back from the dead and defeating Satan!

I didn't understand it; I was a nonbeliever. So why was I so locked into this book? Could it be that this really happened? The things Jesus said to me and showed me were real, so I was starting to see that the Bible was real. I quickly got up and looked into my mirror. *Am I a sinner?* I asked myself. *Did Jesus really die to save us from our sins?* He did pay the price; all we had to do was to believe and receive it.

I thought about that person who bought our drinks at the sports bar that night. He paid the price for our drinks. All we had to do was walk up to the bar and receive our free drinks. I was starting to believe in Jesus. Then I started thinking about the cab driver and his story about going to hell. *Is there really a place like that for the lost?* I thought to myself. The dream when I was engulfed by the fire...*was that hell?* I remember looking into his eyes as he was telling his story. It was as if he was still there. Forever is a long time to be in a place like that. Suddenly, my heart began to soften, and I was starting to believe. I believed that Jesus was real. I wanted to tell Him, so I hurried up and went to sleep, hoping He would come to talk.

I woke up the next morning, disappointed. Jesus did not visit me in my dreams. I pondered why He didn't show up. Maybe He was busy helping someone else, but then I remembered He is omnipresent. I got dressed and went to work.

I could barely focus on my tasks while at work. I wanted to tell someone about my encounters with Jesus. I was so excited. It felt as if blinders had been taken off my eyes.

I was going to see Stacy later on after work and was going to tell her everything. After all, I could trust her. She was going to become my wife someday.

Later that night, I ordered a pizza, and we watched a movie. I could not understand why I was so nervous about telling her.

"What's on your mind, Victor?" Stacy pried. "I can see it on your face."

Apparently, I was wearing my concern on my face. I sighed, took a deep breath, and spoke. "What if I told you that Jesus exists?"

Stacy put down her pizza slice and wiped her hands on a napkin. "This is what's on your mind—Jesus? Enlighten me, why do you suddenly believe He exists? Is it because of the old lady who approached you on your lunch break? Or perhaps it was the man who paid for our dinner?"

"You are not going to believe this, but He came to me in a dream!" I declared.

Stacy burst into laughter. "Okay, now you have really gone off the deep end. Jesus is coming to you in your dreams? That's the dumbest thing I've ever heard!"

"It's true," I maintained. "Jesus really came to me. Why would I make this up?"

I pulled out my Bible and showed her what I had been reading. Stacy quickly snatched it from my hands and threw it across the room.

"Stop it with this nonsense!" she yelled.

"Why are you getting so angry?" I demanded. "I was going to ask you about your anger towards that man in the restaurant, but I thought it was because you were irritated when he came into our conversation."

"No, it was because I don't like Christians and their Bible talk," Stacy retorted. "They think they are better than us. We both used to think the same way, and then I come to your house and you are flashing a Bible in my face!"

"Can I say something now?" I begged.

"Go ahead!" she dared while folding her arms. I walked over and picked up my Bible.

"I saw my great-grandmother in my dream the other night."

"So, what's that got to do with anything?" Stacy challenged.

"She was not old, and she knew who I was."

"Big deal! What's your point, Victor?"

"The point is, she was dead before I was born!"

I took out the picture of my great grandmother and showed it to Stacy. "Her name is Victoria," I started. "I saw this picture of her for the first time yesterday when my mother gave it to me. I never knew what she looked like as a young woman. Victoria came to me in my dream the night before I laid eyes on this picture, and she looked exactly like this!"

Stacy paused for a moment, then she spoke. "Let me get

this straight! Jesus showed you your great-grandmother who died years before you were born?"

"Yes," I sighed.

"And, Jesus, Himself, has been visiting you....in your dreams?"

"Yes, Stacy," I sighed again.

"You believe all of this?" asked Stacy.

I sighed even deeper and pleaded, "I'm being honest with you Stacy! Do you believe me?"

"Well, there's no doubt I believe you," she started. "I believe you have completely lost your stinking mind!" Then Stacy walked to the door saying, "Lose this Jesus guy, or you lose me!" She then left and slammed the door on her way out.

I was left alone in my house with nothing but my thoughts on what just happened. I put the rest of the pizza in the fridge, turned off the TV, and went to bed for the night.

CHAPTER 6

PERSECUTION

****

L ater that week, I met up with my friends, Allen, his girlfriend Sharon, and Johnny to hang out. We were at Allen's house to have one of our round table discussions. Stacy was a no-show; no surprise there with her being upset with me still. Jesus did not visit me either. I was still wondering about that. I wanted to tell Him that I read the book of John. I became so interested in John that I also read Matthew, Mark, and Luke.

To begin our round table discussions, we would take a small, fuzzy handball. We called it "the talking ball." Whoever was holding the ball had control of the topic of which to speak. When the topic was finished, the speaker would toss the fuzzy ball to the next person. If they didn't have a topic to speak on or if they were not ready to speak, they could pass the ball to the next person.

Johnny started first with the talking ball. Johnny, never a person who is short on words, didn't have a topic to speak on yet. He tossed the talking ball over to Allen, who was not ready to speak on his topic yet. He passed the talking ball to Sharon, and she didn't have a topic to speak on either, so she tossed the talking ball to me. I knew what I wanted to speak on—the gospel.

"I know we all don't believe in Jesus, but what if I told you all He was real, and I could prove it?"

Total silence gripped the room. Everyone had a blank stare aimed at me. They all had half smiles, waiting for me to tell them I was joking. After they saw that I was serious, the half- smiles quickly turned into scowls.

"Vic, are you serious?" Allen wondered.

"He's not serious; he's kidding...right?" Sharon insisted.

Johnny shook his head. "I think he's serious, y'all," he resolved with a sigh.

"Come on, hear me out," I begged. "Let me explain."

"Okay, Vic! Entertain us," Sharon challenged. "Let's hear your proof."

I told them everything that happened to me and the scriptures that I read that backed everything Jesus said to me. I even told them about how He came to me in my dreams. I told them about the conversations, but I didn't tell them about how He shut my mouth for a day. Some things you just have to keep to yourself. After I was done, everyone busted out into hysterical laughter.

"Victor is becoming a preacher before our very eyes!" Allen announced.

"So, you don't believe I'm telling the truth?" I marveled.

Johnny got up to speak to the room. "Look y'all, in Victor's defense, he has been getting approached by some extraordinarily strange people the past few weeks. I was there for two of these encounters."

What does that have to do with us?" demanded Sharon. "The fact remains, Jesus does not exist, and that lame story Vic dreamed up does not count as "proof."

"Victor, do you really believe all of this stuff?" Allen probed.

"I have witnessed so much over the past few weeks. It's hard not to believe," I shrugged. "I feel like something inside me is changing, and—I want to allow it to change me."

"Aliens!" Johnny teased.

Everyone looked at Johnny with confused looks.

"It's aliens! I'm convinced the real Victor has been abducted by aliens and they replaced him with this lame version of him!"

Allen and Sharon started laughing.

"I think we need to kick this Victor out and keep him

away until the real Victor comes back."

Johnny then turned and looked at me. "If you are becoming a believer, then why are you hanging out with us nonbelievers?"

"I ... I don't understand what you are saying, Johnny," I explained. "I hang out with you all because we're friends." I looked at Allen and Sharon. "Do you guys want me to leave?" Allen put his head down slightly. Sharon had a smirk on her face and shrugged her shoulders. I turned and looked at Johnny. We had been friends since middle school. He was looking as if I was just some passerby on the street.

"I think we need a break from you and your newfound doctrine, bro," he decided.

I looked him in his eyes, and I saw that he really meant it.

"Maybe you should find yourself a church," Allen joked. "I'm sure you'll find more of your kind there."

They all began to laugh at me as I headed to the door.

"You better pray Stacy is still by your side," Sharon added. "She already told me about your pizza date gone wrong. I'll give her a call; maybe she'll come by since you are leaving now."

I could still hear them laughing at me as I trudged down the hall. I could hear them mocking Jesus' name. It almost angered me, but I remembered how I was before I met Jesus. I was just as bad as they were. I thought back to the scriptures I read about the soldiers who mocked Jesus. Suddenly it dawned on me. Was Jesus showing me what it was like to be a believer?

Many times, my friends and I would mock and ridicule other Christians. Now, I was on the other side of the spectrum. I wasn't even following Jesus at that moment. I was just figuring out things about Him. That still didn't matter to my friends. By the time I made it home, I had realized what kind of a jerk I had been to Christians.

I wondered if Jesus was going to show up in my dreams that night. I needed to talk to someone. I actually felt alone and abandoned. My mother would not have understood because she was not a believer, my friends ridiculed me to shame, and my girlfriend was upset simply because I spoke about Jesus. *Why do people get so riled up when it comes to Jesus?* I thought.

***

Before I went to bed, I called my dad. He didn't believe in Jesus either, but he was there when my great-grandmother died. Perhaps he saw something before she passed away.

My dad picked up the phone, "Hey son, how's it going?"

"I'm doing good, dad," I claimed. "I wanted to talk to you about Grandma Victoria."

"Sure, what do you want to know?"

"Well, is there anything else that happened the night she passed away?" I explored.

My dad thought about it for a second before he spoke. "Well, after she finished speaking all crazy, she looked up to the ceiling, then she looked at me and smiled. I was only 11 years old at the time, so I really didn't think much of it."

"What do you think it meant?" I prodded.

"Son, I don't know! I was a kid," he explained. "Why are you asking?"

"I just wanted to know more about her; that's all," I replied.

"I really didn't get to spend that much time with her," dad continued. "We visited her when we could, about once a year. The next thing I know, we're all standing around her bed, watching her take her final breaths. I really didn't understand everything that was going on until I was older.

"One thing I do miss about grandma is her cooking. She made the best peach cobbler! She would put chunks of dough in it, bigger than normal. Just the way I liked it. Oh, I would do anything to have one more serving."

My dad continued marveling at Grandma Victoria's cooking. *This is going nowhere*, I thought to myself. The only significant thing was that she looked at my dad and smiled at him before she died.

After I got off the phone with my dad, I went to sleep disappointed about the lack of info he provided me regarding Grandma Victoria.

CHAPTER 7

A VISION

****

Several days went by, and my belief in Jesus was stronger, but I was not all in with Him yet. Along the way, I'd lost my friends, and I was okay with that. After all, what kind of friends would ridicule someone because of their personal beliefs? I also realized I was a hypocrite because I was ridiculing people because of their beliefs.

I was still wondering about my relationship with Stacy. It had been a while since we spoke, but I still felt like she would come around, and everything would be ok.

I was still not fully committed to living like a true Christian yet. I was still living the life I wanted to live. I was beginning to embrace the change brewing inside me. I was reading my Bible more and getting an understanding of what

Jesus did. It just wasn't in my heart as of yet.

I was really missing Stacy. I loved her so much. I hated that we hadn't seen each other for so long, so I decided to text, asking her to come over so we could talk things out. Stacy agreed to come by. I knew once we saw each other, everything would work out. I missed her, and I knew she missed me.

Things were a bit awkward at first, but once we both sat down, that feeling went away.

"So, how's it been?" I inquired.

"Fine, I guess," she remarked.

"Did you miss me?"

"It depends," Stacy tested. "Did you drop all of this Jesus talk?"

Stacy looked at the coffee table and saw that I still had my Bible. I picked it up. Stacy got up, went to the kitchen, and brought back the wastebasket. She set it in front of me, expecting me to toss the Bible into the wastebasket.

I loved Stacy so much, but she was placing me in a position where I had to choose between her or Jesus. Then I thought about how my friends treated me when I told them about Jesus. Suddenly, the decision became clear. I had to choose Jesus. I wanted to know more about Him. I knew everything I needed to know about Stacy because of how she was treating me concerning my decision to learn more about Jesus. I also knew what my so-called friends were about. I knew at that point that Stacy was not the one for me, so I moved the wastebasket towards Stacy.

"I'm sorry, but ever since I've met Jesus, I don't think I can turn back. You know, you can come with me on this journey. It's not as bad as you think. In fact, meeting Jesus is actually turning my life around."

Stacy's jaw dropped. Then she let out this fake laugh and leaned back on the couch. "I guess you have made your choice," she reckoned.

Stacy reached behind her neck and removed the necklace I bought her for our six-month anniversary. She placed it on the coffee table and looked at me.

"I'm serious, Vic! I'm done with you if you keep this up!"

I knew right then that that was going to be the end of us. We had been together for well over a year. We were even talking about getting married soon. I was secretly saving up for an engagement ring and was planning to propose to her on our two-year anniversary. When people get married, they sometimes go through changes, for better or for worse. Although my mom and dad were divorced, they told me how they came together during rough times when they were married. I could see now that Stacy would not honor that if we had gotten married. Stacy was not the woman for me, and it hurt me to finally see it.

"If me wanting to know Jesus is all it takes for you to leave me, then leave."

Stacy gasped, got up, and picked up the necklace. She opened the door and turned to speak, "This necklace is going into the creek!" Then she slammed the door shut.

I took a deep breath and came to the realization that Stacy and I were done. I was sad about it, but it showed me what kind of person she really was.

***

The night was still young, and I needed to get some air and a few drinks. I took a walk to the sports bar and had a few beers to drink my sorrows away. A few beers became too many, and I drank myself into a drunken mess. The bartender saw that I had too many beers, so he called me a cab to take me home. I didn't remember getting into a cab or even getting home for that matter. The last thing I remember was flopping onto my bed.

I went to sleep and had a dream that I was at a movie theater. The place was packed full of people. It was very foggy inside, and I could hardly see in front of me. An usher slowly walked by and handed me a pair of 3D glasses. He didn't even look at me as he casually walked by. I turned to the screen, and it was white. There wasn't a movie showing on it yet. I noticed that the other people there were not wearing their 3D glasses; however, they were looking at the screen as if a movie was showing. Out of curiosity, I put my 3D glasses on, and saw some of the most horrific sights I had ever witnessed. I saw demon-like creatures everywhere! They were crawling all over the walls, the ceiling, and even on the people! The people acted as if they didn't see them. In fact, some of the creatures had leashes on them and were attached to some of the people like they were pets!

I quickly took off my glasses and looked around. The demons were gone, but the people were still there. I put the glasses back on, looked around, and saw the demons again. The auditorium was filled with them. They were crawling all over each other and looked slimy and dark-colored. They all had yellow and red eyes. Some had bat-like wings, and others looked like giant rats. Some of them were so horrifically disfigured that I really could not explain to you what they looked like.

I took my 3D glasses off and ran for the exit, but the usher was blocking the door. I told him to get out of my way so I could leave. The usher slowly put his finger to his lips.

"Shhhhhhh! Put your 3D glasses on and read what's on the screen."

I put my glasses back on and walked back to look at the screen. In bold letters that appeared to be written in blood read, WELCOME HOME, VICTOR! As soon as I read it, all of the demons instantly looked at me! They all screamed and lunged at me at the same time! I turned, ran to the exit, and ran into the usher. I realized then that I still had my 3D glasses on. The usher was a demon, too! He grabbed me, and I looked into his creepy, yellow eyes. I tried to shake myself from his grasp, but he was so strong! The demon laughed at me, flashed his claws, and scratched me across my face! At that moment, I was jolted awake!

When I woke up, I was gripped with intense fear. I looked at my clock, and it was only 2:30 in the morning. It was still dark in my room. Although I was by myself, I could feel an evil presence in the room with me. Nervously, I looked around but didn't see anything. Like a scared child, I buried myself under my blanket and tucked my legs close to my chest. I crossed my arms across my chest and lay motionless under my blanket. I was shivering with immense fear for what was lurking in my room. I started to pray quietly, "Jesus, I know You are real. I know You cast out demons when You spoke. Please cast this demonic presence out of my house."

I kept praying that prayer under my blanket until I fell asleep again. I awoke the next morning to a pounding headache, nausea, and a terrible taste of last night's alcohol in my mouth. I saw a business card lying on my nightstand. It had a name on it: *Kyle Austin, Cab Driver*. Hmm, a rather plain card, I said to myself. I flipped the card over, and there was handwriting on the back; it read:

Call me after you take care of your hangover.

You know who I am.

My head was pounding, and the room was spinning. I was hungry and nauseous at the same time. Slowly, I dragged myself to the kitchen to grab a sports drink to refuel. Once the room stopped spinning, I called Kyle Austin. Before I dialed his number, I realized I didn't remember how I got to my house. *How did I get home?* I asked myself. *Did Kyle Austin help me get home and then put his business card on my nightstand?* I figured I was so wasted that Kyle, the cab driver, must have helped me get home and made sure I was in bed safely. "Good man!" I said aloud.

I called Kyle up.

"Hello, Kyle Austin, cab driver. How may I help you?"

"Hello Kyle! You left a business card with a message on it for me to call you."

"Ah, Victor! How are you doing?"

"How did you know my name?" I questioned.

"You told me last night when you were in my cab," Kyle answered.

"Oh, right," I affirmed. I didn't even remember the cab ride home. "Thanks for helping me get home safely last night," I mentioned.

"You're welcome," Kyle remarked. "Hey, are you hungry?"

"Of course, I am," I admitted.

"How about I pick you up in about an hour, and I'll take you to lunch, on me, of course."

"Well, since you are paying, then I guess I have no choice but to take you up on your offer," I agreed. "I'll be ready in an hour."

I wondered where I heard Kyle's voice before as I got off the phone with him. I jumped in the shower and got dressed.

The doorbell rang, and I got up to answer it. I looked into the peephole, and I gasped. I opened the door. "IT'S YOU!" I yelled. "Jesus told me about you!"

Kyle had a confused look on his face.

"I remember you from the cab ride a few weeks ago when you dropped my friend and me off," I explained.

"Yes," Kyle agreed. "So, what were you talking about when you said Jesus told you about me?"

"Come in," I invited.

I was nervous about telling him what I had been going through, but then again, he told us about his visit to hell when he was shot a few years ago. I took a deep breath and told him everything. I told him how Jesus paid me a visit in my dream and how He told me about him after our cab ride a few weeks ago. As I was talking, I could see that he was very interested and was listening intently. When I was finished, he put his hand on my shoulder.

"Young man, I believe every single word you just said."

I gave him a hug.

"Kyle, you are the only one who believes me."

"Then this means you now believe what I told you in my cab a few weeks ago."

"Yes, I believe you," I affirmed. "I've been dreaming

about demons, monsters, and other crazy things I can't even name. It's driving me crazy!"

"Come on and let's eat," Kyle suggested. "You can go more in-depth about your experience while we eat."

After we were done eating, Kyle invited me to church with him. I was skeptical about going at first, but I told him I would go.

"How would I be sure if this is a good church?" I inquired.

Kyle laughed. "After what I went through, finding a good, honest church was paramount to me."

The bill came and I offered to pay. Kyle stopped me and told me he would pay. "You paid for lunch, and the cab ride a few weeks ago," I noted.

"Don't forget about last night when you were too drunk to pay," Kyle added with a smile.

"I'm sorry about that," I apologized.

"I'm not judging you, Victor," Kyle mentioned. "Everyone has their own walk."

Kyle gave me the address to his church and took me back home. As I walked through my door, a shiny flicker caught my eye. It came from my coffee table. I went over to see what it was, and I could not believe it! It was the necklace I had bought for Stacy! I picked it up, looked up, and smiled. I had a feeling that I was going to get another visit from Jesus soon.

CHAPTER 8

CLARITY

****

I went through a lot in the past few weeks. My friends didn't want much to do with me, my breakup with Stacy, even going through the nightmares and visions. In some ways, I was glad to be going to church with Kyle. At least I could take my mind off the things I had gone through.

***

Sunday morning came, and I got dressed and went to church with Kyle. I must admit, I was nervous about going. Kyle assured me that everything would be fine.

"I'm sorry I didn't wear a suit to church," I admitted.

"Yeah, you really angered God by wearing jeans," Kyle replied sarcastically. "God does not look at your outer appearance; it's what is on the inside that matters."

We went inside and sat down, but I felt like everyone was looking at me.

"Relax, Victor! No one is looking at you."

"How did you know I was thinking that?" I marveled.

"Because I was the same way when I first came to church," Kyle commented. "Just take a deep breath and keep an open mind, Victor."

The worship leader told everyone to stand up and give praise as the band began to play. The first two songs were upbeat and lively.

"What part of the church is this?" I inquired.

"This is praise and worship," Kyle explained.

"We are worshiping God right now?" I wondered.

"Yes," Kyle affirmed. "We are thanking Him for just being who He is and what He has done for us."

After the lively songs were done, the lights dimmed, a woman took the stage and began to sing. The song was mellow and soothing. I leaned over to Kyle again.

"Is this still praise and worship?"

"Yes, it is," Kyle remarked. "I want you to close your eyes, feel the music, and let God into your heart. Forget about your problems and your worries, give it all to God, and let Him in."

I closed my eyes and began to focus on God. The song was elegant, and the woman's voice was beautiful. I began to feel the music, then suddenly a gentle presence came over me.

I began to think about what I had read in the Bible. I thought about the compassion Jesus had on those who came to Him. Suddenly, I felt like I was in another place. I was in a very peaceful state. I suddenly felt like something had surrounded me. It was a comforting presence as if someone had come over and put their arms around me to hug me. I felt a release of emotions, and my eyes filled with tears. I didn't know what was happening to me, but I knew I liked it.

The song lasted about ten minutes, but I didn't care. It was so beautifully played; I didn't care if it played for thirty minutes. After worship was done, I leaned over to speak to Kyle.

"Who was that singing? She sounded so good."

"Oh, that was my wife, Candace," Kyle acknowledged with a smile.

"How come you didn't tell me you were married?" I questioned.

"You never asked me," Kyle defended. "I'll introduce you to her in a bit."

While the church announcements played on the big screen, Kyle's wife, Candace, came over and sat next to him.

"Victor, this is my lovely wife, Candace."

I shook her hand. "You have a beautiful voice," I marveled.

"Thank you," she acknowledged. "I'm just using the talent God has blessed me with."

Soon, the sermon began. The pastor preached on repentance. He wasn't one of those screaming pastors that pulled out their handkerchiefs every few minutes and wiped the sweat off their brow. I saw my share of those guys on TV. He was a laid-back kind of person, but you could tell he had a true passion for what he did when he spoke.

"Everyone sitting in here today is a believer," he began, "but not everyone in here is a follower. Turn to Matthew 7:19-20. It says every tree that brings not forth good fruit is hewn down and cast into the fire. Therefore, by their fruits you shall know them."

I remember reading that when I was at home, but I didn't understand it at the time. Now it made sense to me. Some of my church-going friends were not producing fruit as far as I knew. If they continued that way, they would be hewn down and cast into the fire. *That's pretty blunt,* I thought. Later in the sermon, the pastor had us turn to Acts 2:38 and he read, "Then Peter said to them, 'Repent, and be baptized, every one of you, in the name of Jesus Christ for the remission of sins, and you shall receive the gift of the Holy Ghost.'"

The pastor continued, "What does this mean, you ask? Well, let me explain it to you. When you repent, you turn away from your sinful nature. You no longer enjoy those sins, and there is now an effort to put those things in the past. Now, to be baptized is a public showing of you burying the old person and coming out a new person in Christ. Now you are able to receive the Holy Spirit."

"I have to do all of these things to become a Christian?" I prodded.

"If you want to be a true follower of Jesus, then yes," Kyle responded.

That really gave me something to ponder. I was a believer, and that was a fact. However, did I want to commit to all of the other things that came with being a believer? I couldn't answer that question honestly.

After church, Kyle introduced me to a few of his friends. We spoke for a while, and soon it was just Kyle and me in the lobby.

"So, what do you think?" Kyle probed. "Did you like it?"

"Yes, I did," I remarked. "I liked the worship part, and some of the things the pastor said today really stuck with me."

"If you want to come back next week, just let me know," Kyle offered.

Although I liked everything about church that day, I didn't know if I was going to come back.

***

When I got home, I sat in my chair and reviewed some of the scriptures the pastor went over in his message. As I was reading, I fell asleep, and found myself in that familiar room. The room was a little brighter than usual before Jesus would come in.

"Where are You?" I demanded. "There is much to

discuss."

After about a minute, Jesus walked in. "Victor, there you are. There is much to discuss."

"I just said that," I muttered.

"I know, I was just mocking you," Jesus replied with a chuckle.

"Wait, did You just joke with me?" I probed. "You are not supposed to be joking."

"Why not?"

"Because You are Jesus, that's why."

Jesus leaned back and laughed. "Victor, I enjoy watching My children have good clean fun. They make Me laugh sometimes, as well."

"Wow, I never knew that," I marveled. "I read the book of John just like You told me."

"I know you did," Jesus affirmed. "I'm pleased because you also read the other books of the gospel as well. Could it be that you are getting interested in My Word?"

I smiled. "I guess You can say that!"

I thought about my friends, turned away, and looked down. "My friends have distanced themselves from me, and my girlfriend broke up with me because of my belief in You."

"My child, many of My followers have gone through the same thing you are now going through. Husbands have divorced wives, wives have divorced husbands, parents have disowned their children, and the list goes on. The majority of this world will hate you because of Me, but like I said in John 15:18, 'Know that the world hated Me before it hated you.'"

Instinctively, I reached for my Bible to look at the scripture. I soon realized that my Bible was not there. Jesus handed me a Bible that appeared to have come out of nowhere. It was already opened, and the scripture was highlighted. I read it to get a better understanding of it.

"I remember reading this," I motioned.

"The people who you think are your friends will show their true colors when it comes to Me," Jesus began. "In this case, your friends just showed you how you used to be."

I put my head down in shame. "I was a complete knucklehead, and I won't be like that again."

"All has been forgiven at the cross," Jesus comforted.

"I had a nightmare I wanted to ask You about," I started.

Jesus listened intently as I went into detail about the nightmare I had experienced. After I was done telling Him, He interpreted my dream.

"That was not a nightmare, My son, but a vision. The movie theater was the world; the people in the theater were the people of the world. Your 3-D glasses symbolized spiritual discernment, meaning you got a glimpse of how demons operate in the spirit realm. The reason why the people didn't wear their 3-D glasses was because they didn't have nor cared to have the sight. The people who had leashes attached to some of the demons were the ones who knew they were sinning, yet they enjoyed their sins. They did not want to let them go."

I was amazed that my nightmare revealed much more than what I saw.

"All of this is happening in the world today?" I questioned.

"Yes, it is," Jesus admitted.

"There was "Welcome Home, Victor" on the big screen. What did that mean?" I urged.

"Satan wants you to perish with him," Jesus chimed in. "When I rose from the dead, Satan knew his days were numbered. He's in a sinking ship, and his sole mission is to take as many people as he can with him."

"I felt an evil presence in the room with me after I woke up. Was that Satan?"

"No, it was one of his demons assigned to you," Jesus explained.

"Wait, so You knew that demon was in the room with me and You didn't do anything, why?"

Jesus sighed, "I was there with you, but you were focused on the evil presence and your fear, not Me. The moment you prayed for Me to cast that evil spirit out, I did. How do you think you went back to sleep? I gave you peace."

"Oh, my goodness!" I exclaimed. "You really were there! I was wondering how I went to sleep so quickly!"

"Victor, I never left you, nor will I ever leave you," Jesus soothed. "I knew you before you were even born. You still have a lot to learn about Me. Don't worry, my child; I will be here whenever you need Me. Our time here is finished; it's time for you to wake up."

Instantly, I was awake. I looked down at my Bible in my lap. I saw that it was in the book of John, chapter 15. Verses 18 and 19 suddenly became highlighted. Jesus made sure I would not forget it because when I dozed off, I had my Bible opened to Acts 2:38.

CHAPTER 9

DISTANT FRIENDS

****

I was at the local diner, grabbing a bite to eat when I saw Johnny walk in with a new girlfriend. I could see him roll his eyes once he saw me. However, since we've been best friends since middle school, I guess he felt he had to come over to talk.

"How's it going, Vic?" he mumbled.

"Fine," I answered.

"Oh, this is Michelle," Johnny introduced.

"Hi Michelle, it's nice to meet you," I acknowledged.

Michelle turned to Johnny and inquired, "Is that the Bible fanatic you were talking about?"

Johnny's face reddened. "No ... that's another guy I was talking about."

I knew Johnny was lying. I was the fanatic he was

talking about. Michelle went to the ladies' room and Johnny sat at my table.

"So, what's going on with you, bud?" he explored. "I haven't seen you since..."

"Y'all kicked me out!" I interrupted.

I was still quite upset about that. I was so embarrassed and humiliated that night.

"Oh, yeah," Johnny moaned. "Listen, bro, I'm sorry about how that went down. It's just ... you know, I was getting annoyed with all of that Jesus this and Jesus that. I had enough of it. We miss you, Vic. Stacy misses you, too. She won't admit it, but we all can see it in her face. Come back, bro."

"I can't, not after all the things I've seen," I countered. "Johnny, maybe it's time you start looking at the way you have been living your life. Jesus is real, and He's calling out to you. Don't ignore Him. At least listen to Him. He's not going to force you. Just hear what He wants to say to you. What do you say?"

Johnny looked at me in bewilderment. "Bro, you really did go off on the deep end! I thought you were going through a phase or something, but you really are taking this Jesus thing to a completely new level! I don't even know who you are anymore! Who do you think you are to judge me? I'm a grown man, and I can do whatever I want! I don't need you or your Jesus to tell me how to live my life!"

I had never seen Johnny get so angry like that before. It was as if he was temporarily possessed. Then I saw something behind Johnny! It was a demon, and it was looking right at me! I only saw it for a split second, but it was long enough to see what it looked like. It had a dark and sinister look on its face and was scowling at me! I quickly rubbed my eyes, looked again, and it was gone. Johnny's demeanor appeared to have changed as well. He didn't appear angry anymore, either.

Michelle came out of the ladies' room, and Johnny got up.

"We're going over to sit at the booth; I'll catch up with you later, Vic."

"Johnny, come to church with me on Sunday," I pleaded. "Just one Sunday, please?"

Johnny paused and turned around. He placed both hands on the table, leaned in close to my face, and looked me right into my eyes. "I will never go to church with you, and I will never listen to that fake god you call Jesus."

Johnny straightened up, and he and Michelle walked to the booth. I paid for my lunch, and I left. As I was driving home, I was thinking about that hideous face that was behind Johnny. I've seen some weird things the past few weeks, but that was the first time I saw something that creepy while I was awake. I knew it was a demon, but how could I see it, and no one else could? I thought about my vision in that creepy movie theater. There were people who were connected to demons with a leash. Those people didn't want to let go of certain sins. Could Johnny be holding on to something that he did not want to let go of? Whatever it was that was behind Johnny, it was angry at me for trying to talk to him about Jesus.

***

Although I wasn't going to church every Sunday, Kyle and I still kept in touch. I asked him to pray for my friends because I was praying for them to get saved even though I was not officially saved myself.

I had grown in my knowledge of the Bible, as far as the gospels. I had book knowledge, but it wasn't in my heart yet. To me, it just made sense to be a believer. I wanted my friends to become believers as well, but that was going to be a tall mountain to climb.

Occasionally, I would see Allen and Sharon when I was out. They would walk by without uttering a single word to me. I found out from an acquaintance that Stacy had moved on and found another boyfriend. I think he hated Jesus even more than Stacy did. Johnny probably outdid them all when it came to distancing themselves from me. He unfriended me from all of his social media accounts, blocked my phone number, and told his mom that I was dead to him. Johnny's mom and my mom were good friends, so I wasn't completely cut off from him.

I would reckon this was why some people don't stick

and stay with Jesus when they become a believer. I was the total opposite. If my friends were acting like that towards me, then I would want to follow Jesus even more. It's not like He was lying and stealing from people. He healed the sick, cast out demons, and He died on the cross to save us from our sins. He was the Son of God. I would rather be on His side anyway, especially after all the things I had been through at this point.

***

Kyle invited me to come over for dinner at his house. I was hesitant at first, but he told me that his wife insisted, and would not take no for an answer. Kyle gave me his address and told me to be there on Saturday at 1 pm. My intention was not to stay long. I'm sure they were good people; I just didn't know them well.

I was barely out of my car when I began to smell the food. I saw Kyle sitting on his porch.

"Victor, it's good to see you. Come on in!"

He took me to the back yard where Candace was.

"Hi, Victor, how are you?"

"I'm fine, Mrs. Austin," I nodded.

"Please, call me Candace," she objected with a smile. "Mrs. Austin is my mother."

Kyle brought me a lawn chair. "Have a seat, young man," he offered.

Candace brought me a pop to drink and a plate. "Dig in; there's plenty more if you want."

I took one look at my plate: two brats, mac and cheese, potato salad, and a huge slice of cheesecake. I responded, "Trust me, I think this is more than plenty for me!"

"Have you had any more visits from Jesus?" Kyle inquired.

"I have, but it's been a while," I answered.

"You know, Victor, Jesus comes to us in many different ways, but I never heard of Him coming to people like He's done with you."

"I think it's wonderful!" Candace gleamed with a big smile. "It just goes to show you that our God will go out of His way to get His message across."

"I have learned so much since He visited me," I shared.

"I'm glad you are getting to know him," Kyle chimed in. "Did you get saved yet?"

"No, not yet," I stammered.

Kyle and Candace both scowled at me with confused looks on their faces. "What are you waiting for?" Kyle challenged.

"I don't know," I shrugged. "I guess I need more time to figure things out."

"I don't understand," Kyle burst out. "Jesus came to you ... and spoke to you. What's more to discuss?"

"I'm not ready to dive all the way into this yet," I fretted. "I believe Jesus knows this. He wants me to make this decision on my own. I think Jesus wants to show me more things before I make my choice."

"Young man, you have been given a rare opportunity to get a visit from Jesus Christ in person," Candace chorused. "Not too many people on record have actually laid eyes on Him since His ascension to Heaven in the New Testament. It would be a shame to waste this golden opportunity! Please, don't blow it. There are people in hell right now that rejected Christ countless times. They had many opportunities to get saved, and now they are spending eternity regretting their decisions."

"My mind says to weigh all of my options before I commit," I resolved.

"What does your heart say?" Kyle hinted.

"My heart says to take the leap of faith," I clarified.

"Victor, we do not want to put any added pressure on you," Candace explained. "Ultimately, it will be your decision to make because God has given us free will to choose."

I nodded in agreement.

"I have seen the change in me so far," I agreed. "I was a non-believer who became a believer. I just need more time to take that next step, I guess."

"I'm going to level with you, Victor," Kyle began. "Before I got shot that night, I believed in God. I wasn't saved, nor did I follow Him like I do today. I lived a very worldly life. I was a proud sinner. I partied, drank, and I fornicated...."

Kyle reached over and gently gripped Candace's hand,

"...and I was committing adultery. The demons that were tormenting me were the same ones that were encouraging me to commit all of those sins. They told me this while they were tormenting me. They were assigned to me from Satan. They placed all the temptations in front of me, and I gave in to just about all of them. You see Victor, it's their job to make sure we all stay away from God because Satan wants us to perish with him in the lake of fire. I thank God every day because He gave me a second chance.

"I know what it's like to beg for Jesus to save me and not hear His voice. I know what it is like to have my soul completely engulfed in eternal flames, tormented by demons, and have my regrets about my sinful life at the same time. I've told many people about this, and I can tell some of them didn't believe me. Many of them were Christians."

While Kyle spoke, I could see the emotion in his face. It was the same look on his face when he first spoke to Johnny and me in the cab that night. I could tell he and his wife cared about not just me, but people altogether. We only knew each other for a short time, yet he was so open to me about his personal life. I could clearly see that Kyle and his wife cared deeply about me.

After we finished eating, I helped them put away the food, put away the lawn chairs, fold the picnic table, and then we went inside.

"Thank you for having me over; the food was

delicious."

"Thank you, Victor," Candace shot back. "You are welcome to come over anytime. You are family now."

As I was leaving, I noticed a family portrait on the wall. It was Kyle and Candace, and it looked to be their son in the portrait as well. Next to the picture was a framed obituary of the same young man who was in the family portrait. I wanted to ask about it, but I thought better of it and continued on my way out.

Sitting on my couch at home, I kept thinking about what Kyle and Candace both said to me. Eventually, I was going to have to make a decision. I was on the fence. I was a believer in Jesus, yet I still wanted to live the life I wanted to live. I also knew I didn't want to go to hell. As I was pondering these thoughts, my mom called me.

"Victor!" she quivered, in a panicky voice.

"What is it, Mom?" I perked up.

"I just got off the phone with Johnny's mom! Johnny has been in a horrible car accident! He's at the hospital in critical condition!"

Hastily, I got up, ran out the door, and rushed to the hospital.

CHAPTER 10

AN ENCOUNTER AT THE HOSPITAL

****

I sped on the freeway getting to the hospital. I had tears running down my face and they blurred my vision as I drove. I had hundreds of thoughts racing through my head. *How bad was he hurt? Who was at fault? Is he going to make it? Was there anyone else in the car with him?*

I made it to the emergency room and saw Johnny's parents. His mother was crying uncontrollably, so I went over to hug her.

"Victor!" she sobbed, "I wish Johnny were hanging out with you tonight instead."

"What happened?" I probed.

She tried to speak but became so overcome with emotion that she collapsed to the floor. Johnny's dad came over and helped me pick her up and take her back to her chair. Johnny's dad sat down next to me after his wife had calmed down

"Victor, Johnny and his girlfriend were out drinking earlier, and he got behind the wheel. He lost control of the car, swerved, and crashed head-on into a semi-truck. His girlfriend was killed instantly, as she took the brunt of the impact."

Tears filled my eyes again as he was telling me this. "How is Johnny?" I asked nervously.

"Not too good," his father sighed. "The doctors are saying that he might not make it. They are still working on him."

I got up and slowly began to pace back and forth across the room. I sat back down in my chair and put my head in my hands. Johnny's dad came back over, sat next to me, and put his hand on my shoulder.

"I know you and he were at odds recently," he softly explained, "but Johnny had no better friend than you."

I held my emotions in check as long as I could. I looked over at Johnny's mother, and she was nodding in agreement with her husband. I finally broke down and began to cry.

"If only you were with him, Victor," his mother cried. "I know we wouldn't even be here because you are careful. I know you would not have let him get behind the wheel drunk."

Johnny's mom was right. Anytime when Johnny and I

went out, if we had drinks, I would make sure that we had a ride. If we didn't, then I would call a cab, or we would walk if it was close.

My mother arrived at the hospital a short time later. She hugged me and asked me if I was okay.

"Not really," I shrugged. "Everything is so unreal right now."

My mother kissed me on my forehead. "We will get through this rough time together," she comforted, then she went to console Johnny's mom. Shortly after, Johnny's dad came back over to talk to me.

"Is it true that the reason why Johnny stopped talking to you is because you found Jesus?"

I nodded.

"Well, that's just stupid that he stopped being your friend because you found religion," he added.

"I never wanted it to be like this," I expressed.

"I know, Victor. Right now, my son needs prayer to help him get through this."

"Are you a Christian?" I inquired.

"Not really," he murmured, "but I know there is a God up there … somewhere."

The doctor came out and called Johnny's parents over. I couldn't hear them talking, but I saw Johnny's dad hug his wife, and they both had slight smiles on their faces. They both walked over to address the family.

"The doctor said Johnny is in a coma," his father explained. "They said it is hard to tell right now. He's in critical but stable condition. Only a couple of us can see him right now, but only for a few minutes.

Everyone agreed that Johnny's parents should only go in to see him.

"Victor, we want you to come with us," his father beckoned.

"No, you two go! I'll wait out here," I rebutted.

"You two are close," his mother insisted. "Come with us."

I got up and looked at my mother. She smiled at me with tears flowing down her cheeks. She motioned me to go with them.

"It's okay; we'll be out here waiting for you," she assured.

***

The walk to Johnny's room seemed to last forever. The initial shock about his accident had worn off, and the reality of it had now set in. I needed to pray for Johnny. His salvation depended on it. I barely knew what that was about, but I knew Johnny needed it. I wanted to pray over him so he could make a full recovery. I didn't know what to say because I had never prayed for someone before, especially someone who was in a coma. The only thing I knew was I had to pray for my best friend.

We finally made it to Johnny's room. We could barely recognize him with all of the tubes and bandages that were all over his body. His swollen face was littered with lacerations and abrasions from the shattered glass. Johnny's mother took one look at her son and buried her face into her husband's chest. Her muffled cry filled the room. I walked over to get a closer look. The machine connected to Johnny beeped in the distance. Johnny's parents came over behind me and I stepped aside to let them see their son.

"Johnny, please wake up," his mother sobbed. "I don't know what I'm going to do if I lose you."

"We brought Victor with us, son," his father added.

I leaned over Johnny, and I gently placed my hand on his shoulder. I began to pray for him.

"Jesus, please help my friend get through this. Heal him just like You healed the people in the Bible. Show Yourself to him and give him a chance to get to know You."

After I prayed, I hugged Johnny's parents and went back to the waiting room.

Most of Johnny's family had gone home by the time I returned to the waiting room. I told my mother I was going to stay overnight with Johnny's parents. Soon after, Johnny's parents came out into the waiting room to get some rest. My mother had a few encouraging words for them, and then she went home. It was only the three of us in the waiting room at that point, and I knew it was going to be a long night, so I decided to take a nap. It was a very uncomfortable chair to be sleeping in. After a few moments of making subtle adjustments, though, I finally went to sleep.

I dreamed I was in Johnny's room in the hospital. The room was darker than usual, but a dim light shone on Johnny. As I walked closer, I could see that he was awake.

"Johnny, can you hear me?"

Johnny looked over at me and groaned, "Yeah, where am I?"

"You're in the hospital," I answered. "You've been in a serious car accident and are in a coma right now. The doctors don't know if you are going to live or die."

Bewildered and with a frown on his face, Johnny questioned, "How am I in a coma if I am talking to you?"

"Call out to Jesus, Johnny," I urged, "ask Him to save you before it's too late."

"Victor, please stop talking to me about Jesus," Johnny sighed. "I'm in the hospital. I'm sure the doctors will patch me up, and I'll be on my way."

While Johnny was speaking, two shadowy figures came out of the shadows on the wall and slowly walked towards him. He saw them and tried to get up, but even in my dream, Johnny was in bad shape. He still had the same injuries in my dream, as he did when I was awake. I tried to run and get Johnny, but one of the figures held out one of his long, bony hands, and instantly I became paralyzed! Once it saw I was frozen in my tracks, it turned its attention back to Johnny. They stood over his bed, and I could see the fear in Johnny's face. He tried to yell, but one of the creatures held out his hand, and Johnny lost his ability to speak. The creatures snatched his blanket off, and they began to beat on Johnny's already broken body. I watched in horror as they beat him for what seemed like minutes non-stop. Actually, I was surprised to see that Johnny survived a beating like that. Just then, one of the creatures grabbed Johnny by his legs and began to drag him towards the wall that they came through. They went through the shadow in the wall, and I could no longer see Johnny. He was gone!

The other creature was halfway through the wall before he stopped. Slowly, he turned around and began to walk towards me! I tried with all of my might to move, but I was still paralyzed. The creature was standing in front of me, face to face.

"We got to Johnny before you did, Victor," it snickered with a laugh.

Suddenly I could hear Johnny from behind the walls screaming. "Somebody help me!!!!"

I began to cry when I heard the creatures tormenting Johnny. The creature turned to look at the wall then he turned slowly back towards me.

"Music to my ears," he taunted with a low growl. Then the shadowy creature raised his hand and swiped across my face. I awoke in a cold sweat!

I looked up and saw the doctor talking to Johnny's parents. Johnny's mother collapsed to the floor, and his father kneeled down with her. Both of them were sobbing uncontrollably.

"I'm sorry, we did everything we could to save him," the doctor conceded.

I knew Johnny had died after hearing the doctor say that. My heart dropped, and my body went limp. I could not believe it. Johnny was dead. I asked Jesus to save him, and He didn't. What's worse, I dreamed he went to hell right before I woke up.

I became angry with Jesus because I prayed and expected Him to answer my prayers. I paced back and forth, trying to contain my emotions. I sat back down in the chair, put my head in my hands, and began to sob. My best friend was gone, and I had a feeling he was not with Jesus in paradise.

"Go home, Victor, and get some rest," Johnny's father expressed. "We appreciate you staying here with us. There is nothing any of us can do now but go home."

I didn't want to go home. I wanted to know why Jesus did not answer my prayers. Why did Johnny have to die?

Johnny's parents urged me to go home, and since they were leaving, I finally decided to go. It didn't make sense for me to be at the hospital if they were leaving. When I got home,

I fell to the floor and cried. I cried so hard it was as if my stomach was forcing the sadness out of me.

"Why did You let him die?" I screamed. I cried myself to sleep right in front of my front door in a pool of tears.

I woke up later that afternoon and checked my phone. My mother had called, my father called, and Johnny's parents called. I didn't return any of the calls. I didn't feel like talking to anyone at the moment. I just wanted to sit in my house, away from everyone. I just wanted to be alone. I barely ate. All I could do was turn on the TV and didn't even watch it. I just needed the noise from it.

Kyle called, and I answered the phone.

"How's it going, Victor? I just wanted to know if you wanted to grab a bite to eat. It's on me, of course."

"Now is not a good time, Kyle," I exhaled. "My best friend passed away early this morning."

"Oh, I'm so sorry to hear that," Kyle acknowledged. "I'll give you some time to grieve, and I'll get in touch with you at a time that's convenient for you."

"Thank you," I replied.

"If you need anything from us, you let us know, okay? Candace and I will be praying for God to comfort you during this trying time."

After I got off the phone with Kyle, I called my mom and dad to let them know how I was coping. Then I called Johnny's parents to see if they needed anything. They were fine; they wanted to make sure I was okay. I really was not but told them I was just so they wouldn't worry about me.

Over the next few days, I spent my time at work, at the bar, and at home. I didn't get a visit from Jesus, nor did I read my Bible. I was broken into pieces over Johnny's death and didn't know how I was going to get over it.

Johnny's father sent a text to tell me that Johnny's funeral was going to be that Saturday. I didn't know if I wanted to attend because I had never been to a funeral before. I had seen a bunch of them on TV, and they looked so sad and gloomy.

I didn't get much sleep since Johnny died. When I did, I kept seeing images of my best friend being dragged off by those demon-like creatures. It was so disturbing to think that Johnny might be in hell, but it was only a dream. Only Johnny and God knew.

CHAPTER 11

THE FUNERAL

* *

I woke up early Saturday morning to get dressed for Johnny's funeral. I had a few drinks the night before but didn't get drunk. The last thing I needed was to be sitting at a funeral with a hangover.

I later arrived at the church and people were already parading inside to find their seats. At a glance, the outside of the church looked as if it had been built centuries ago. When I went inside, though, I could see that it was nothing like the church Kyle invited me to. This church had an eeriness to it. The windows had creepy images painted on them and there were weird paintings on the ceiling.

I looked towards the front, and there I saw Johnny's casket, surrounded by flowers. A few feet from the pulpit, there stood a giant, wooden cross with a sculpture of Jesus on it. This entire church reminded me of a museum.

As I made my way to my seat, I saw my mother come in, and we sat together. I looked around, and all I could feel was utter sadness. I had a feeling that that church would have been sad even if there weren't a funeral here. Soon, the service began. The choir came up to sing, and they, too, sounded weird. I tried to close my eyes to let God in just as I did at Kyle's church, but nothing happened. I leaned over to my mother.

"What kind of church is this?" I inquired.

"I don't know," she answered.

"This place gives me the creeps," I concluded.

A few minutes later, the priest came up to speak about Johnny. He was dressed in a white, baggy robe that had two crosses on either side of his chest. He spoke about Johnny, and the first thing I noticed was his voice. It was low and mundane. His speech was so boring and plain that I started falling asleep. I looked around and saw several people dozing off as well. Even my mother was fighting off the slumber.

Two hours passed, and I could sense the priest was coming to the end of the funeral. Thank goodness! The people in the church began to wake up and the sadness slowly filled the atmosphere again. The choir started to sing a depressing song as we all formed a line to pay our final respects to Johnny. Johnny's mother began to sob as she leaned over to kiss her son's forehead for the last time. His father consoled her as tears streamed down his face.

Soon, my mom and I were standing over Johnny's casket. I studied his lifeless features. His face was pale, and it was caked with loads of foundation, perhaps to cover his facial lacerations from the crash. His hair was styled in a way that he would never have approved if he were alive. That was not the Johnny that I knew, and I could not accept that deceased version of my best friend.

My mother wiped away her tears as she said goodbye to Johnny. I could not take the sadness any longer. I became so overwhelmed with emotion that I ran out of the church, got in my car, and drove home.

With all of the sadness stuffed in that creepy church, the sight of Johnny's lifeless body, and knowing all that I knew from the spiritual side, it was just too much for me to handle. I began to refocus my anger toward Jesus. Once again, He was a no-show when I was going through a difficult time. *Why was that?* I mused. Surely, there had to be an explanation for this.

When I got home, I sat on my couch and turned on my TV. After a short while, I was fast asleep. I dreamed I was in an elevator that was already going up. The elevator suddenly stopped, and I saw that I was on the 13th floor. I felt this cold chill creep up my spine, and fear suddenly crept in. The elevator door wasn't open yet, but I was already afraid of what was on the other side. Slowly, the door began to slide open. I quickly ran to the back of the elevator, crouched into a ball in the corner, buried my face into my hands, and closed my eyes very tightly. I heard footsteps walking towards me, and then a calm voice called out to me, "Give Me your hand."

Gripped with fear, I didn't move or acknowledge the voice. The voice spoke out again to me, "Give Me your hand; it's okay."

With my eyes still closed, I slowly reached out my hand in the direction of the calmed voice. When He grabbed my hand, all of my fear instantly vanished! I remember standing up, but I was so light on my feet, it felt as though I was floating. The man who helped me up was dressed as a hotel manager.

"My name is Emanuel," He declared. "I'm here to show you something, but we don't have much time."

We stepped out of the elevator and into this elegant room. In the room, there was a great, big dining table stretched so far that it seemed to have no end to it. Just above the table hung a chandelier made of pure diamonds. It, too, went as far as I could see. People were sitting at the table. The men were dressed in all-white suits, and the women were wearing elegant dresses. Everyone sitting at the table was young and spry looking, aged between 18-25 years old. Every seat was filled all the way down the table until I could no longer see. As I approached the table, the people focused their attention on me. Everyone was smiling at me.

"Hello Victor!" they all greeted in unison.

"Hi Mark, Carrie, Jan, Mary..." I kept going on and on,

naming everyone sitting at the table. *How did I know all these people by name?* I wondered.

"Here, everyone knows each other by name," Emanuel explained.

I noticed there was one vacant seat. "Why is that seat empty?" I inquired.

Emanuel smiled. "That is your seat."

Suddenly, I felt this wave of joy fill my entire body. It was something I had never felt before. I was experiencing confidence, joy, peace, and happiness all at the same time. I quickly walked towards my seat at the table, but Emanuel put His hand on my shoulder and stopped me.

"You can't sit there yet," He advised. "It's not your time, and you don't have on the proper attire to sit here."

I glanced down to look at myself, and I was dressed in jeans and a black t-shirt. As soon as I saw how I was dressed, I woke up. Unlike the other dreams I had, I understood this one.

The elegant room was heaven. The well-dressed people were the ones who were already in heaven. I wasn't allowed to sit at the table because I wasn't clothed in Jesus' righteousness yet. *How the heck did I know this??* Not a second went by after I asked myself that, I passed out on the floor.

It was total darkness for a minute, then I heard a loud, vacuum, whooshing sound, and then I could suddenly see. I was still in my living room, but I was confused and a bit disoriented. When I finally got my senses back, I looked down, and gasped! I was looking at my own body lying on the floor! I looked at my hands, and they were transparent. "What's going on?" I yelled.

Jesus suddenly appeared to me. "Peace, be still," He comforted.

Instantly, I became calm.

"Victor, I have come to show you something."

"What's happened to me?" I demanded.

"I took your soul from your body," Jesus responded. "We are going to a place where your human body will not survive. You have to go in the spirit, but have no fear, for I will be with you."

"Where are we going?" I pressed.

"I am going to take you to see hell," Jesus responded. "Do you trust Me?"

"I have no choice but to trust You," I shrugged. "I'm standing outside of my body, and I can see through myself, YES, I TRUST YOU!"

"Take My hand," Jesus motioned.

I slowly placed my hand in His, and instantly we were in outer space. I could see the earth from a distance. There were dark, smoky, tornado-like tubes coming out from different parts of the earth.

"Why are those tubes coming from the earth?" I questioned.

"Those are the gateways to hell," Jesus explained. "We are going to go inside one of those tubes to enter hell."

We drew near to one of the tubes and began to descend very rapidly, but it didn't feel like we were falling. Finally, we made it to the ground. When we landed, I noticed a few demon-like creatures scurrying away because of the light that was coming from Jesus. The second thing I noticed was the awful smell of the place. It smelled like rotten eggs and decaying flesh. I could hear agonizing screams of people in the distance. I could hear them yelling, screaming, weeping, and pleading. At that moment, I forgot how upset I was with Jesus. In fact, I drew closer to Him because I did not want Him to leave me.

Jesus knew my thoughts and spoke, "Victor, I know you are upset with Me because you didn't think I was there for you at your worst times. I was there for you. I heard your prayers for Johnny, and I reached out to him to save him just as you asked. Even while he was in his coma, he rejected Me."

"Is Johnny here in this place?" I reluctantly asked.

Although I could barely see Jesus' face, I could tell He was heartbroken.

"Yes, he is, Victor," He moaned. "It saddens me to come here and to hear everyone crying out to Me. I do not send them here, Victor; they send themselves here. Satan and his demons work around the clock, deceiving people, and they allow them to do it. Then when they die, they come to this horrible place of torment. Many of them say they didn't know, but they do know. I show them the exact times they rejected Me. I still love them, even in this place, but there is nothing I can do because judgment is set for them."

"If you still love them, then why do You keep them here?" I challenged.

"Because I paid the price to keep them from coming here," Jesus answered. "All they had to do was accept My free gift of salvation and everlasting life. They refused under their own free will. Others said they would do it later, but they died before they could repent and turn their lives around... another trick of Satan. He had them believing that they could have all the fun the world could provide now, and then when they get old, they would repent, but Satan found ways to kill them before they could repent, and now they are here.

"Many of them simply didn't believe in Me, and they rejected Me when I sent people to talk to them about the gospel. The gospel is the good news, Victor. The good news is you don't have to come to a place like this because I provided a way to avoid it. I gave My life to save every single person from this place of torment."

Jesus put His head down, and He wept. "Yet, there are more people being tormented here than living in paradise with My Father and Me."

Just watching Jesus weeping made me cry as well.

"Come with Me," Jesus invited. "I want to show you one

more thing before we leave here."

Jesus took me to a place that looked like a valley. It was dark and gloomy. There was barely a sky because of the darkness that surrounded it. This place went on for miles. In the valley, there were pits and fire spewed out of the pits at designated times. The stench of this place was unbearable. Jesus took me to one of the pits and told me to look inside it. I could see an older man sitting at the bottom of the pit. It was too dark to see, so I could not make out what he looked like. I just knew he was old. When he saw me, he quickly got up and reached up towards me.

"Quick, help me out of here before it starts up again!" The old man then saw Jesus, and he began to sob. "Jesus, I know I didn't believe in You when I was alive, but I believe now! Please have mercy on me and take me out of here!"

"Judgement is set on you," Jesus clarified. "It's is too late for you."

Jesus then turned and spoke to me, "Do you not recognize him?"

"No, I don't know who that is," I answered.

Jesus stretched out His hand towards the pit, and it became illuminated. I looked into the pit again, and realized it was my great-grandfather! It was Victoria's husband! I knew who he was because of the pictures my mother had of him.

"He rejected Me despite my pleas and Victoria's pleas," Jesus informed. "He believes in Me now, but it is too late for him."

The fire began to rise up in my great-grandfather's pit, and soon it consumed him. The screams I heard coming from him still play in the back of my mind to this very day.

"Jesus, please take me back," I sobbed. "I can't take any more of this."

"I will take you back now," Jesus resolved. "I will come back to bring you here again when the time is right."

Jesus brought me back to my house in an instant. He motioned me to enter my body, which was still lying on the floor. I entered my body and awoke with a gasp of air. I could feel cool air entering my lungs as I took my first human breath in what seemed like hours. I immediately cried out, "Thank You, Jesus!"

As soon as I said that, I remembered that Jesus told me the next time I thanked Him, I would mean it. As difficult of a time I was having at that moment, I managed to muster up a half- smile knowing that I really meant it now, and His Word had come to pass.

***

One week had passed since Johnny's funeral. I slowly began to work myself back into my usual routines again. Occasionally, I would think about what I saw in hell. My great-grandfather was in torment in that horrible place, and there was no rest for him. Then I thought about Johnny. Although I didn't see him, he was down there somewhere as well. There was no way I could tell his parents that. It was hard enough for them as parents to bury their son. They would be devastated to find out that he was in eternal damnation. Now I understood how my great-grandmother felt after Jesus told her that my great-grandfather had perished. Although it broke my heart to have that knowledge of their fates, Jesus did give them many chances to come to Him, and with their own free will, they rejected Him.

Kyle called to see if I wanted to come over. It had been a while since we spoke, so I decided to come by. Kyle and Candace hugged me and told me that if I needed anything, they would be there for me.

"I owe you an apology," I began. "I didn't mean to come across as being rude."

"I know you are a good kid," Kyle offered. "I know all too well about going through something as difficult as losing someone."

"We have something we'd like to tell you, Victor," Candace began. "When my husband first saw you and your friend in his cab, he told me you reminded him of our son. I didn't believe it at first, but when I finally met you, I could see what he was talking about. I can actually say that you remind me of Erick."

"Does he live nearby?" I inquired. "I'd like to meet him."

"Our son, Erick, died two years ago in a boating

accident," Candace sighed. "His body was never found."

"I'm sorry to hear that," I consoled.

"We took his loss pretty hard, but it brought us closer together," Candace mentioned as she held Kyle's hand. "You just remind me so much of him, I don't know if it's a gift or a curse."

"I believe God allowed our paths to cross so we can teach you how to be a true follower of Christ," Kyle added.

"You think so?" I questioned.

"God told me He was going to put me in a position to mentor someone," Kyle explained. "I thought it was going to be someone in our church. Even when I came over to take you out to lunch, I didn't think it was you."

"We know Jesus is working on you, Victor," Candace complemented. "We can see it. We are not going to get in His way, either."

Kyle smiled at his wife, adding, "That's right, Victor. There will be no pressure whatsoever. Whenever you are ready, we will be here for you."

"If you have any questions, feel free to ask us," Candace offered.

I thanked them and then I headed home. While I was driving home, a smile came across my face. I finally had some people who I could talk to about my walk with Christ. I felt like God had placed them in my path just for this very reason. I loved and respected my parents with all of my heart. No one can ever replace them, but I needed someone who could teach me how to walk in the way Jesus would want me to walk, and I had that in Kyle and Candace.

CHAPTER 12

ALLEN'S ENCOUNTER

****

I was at the sports bar watching some games and having a few drinks when I saw Allen come in. I hadn't seen him since that time he and Sharon ignored me. I went over to talk to him.

"What's up, Allen?"

Allen nervously acknowledged me. "Nothing much, Vic," he mumbled.

"Where's Sharon?" I inquired.

"We're not together anymore," Allen stated.

"Sorry to hear that," I empathized. "You two belong together."

"Yeah, well, we're not together; it's over," Allen snapped.

I noticed Allen looked unusually unkempt. He hadn't

shaved in what looked like weeks. He really looked like he was in a somber state.

"You want to tell me what's really going on, bro?" I probed.

Allen took me outside to talk in private. He took a slow, deep breath. "It's all my fault, Vic," he started. "I have to live with this guilt for the rest of my life."

"What are you talking about?" I asked curiously. "Is this about you and Sharon?"

"No," Allen shouted. "It's about Johnny and me! I'm the reason he died that night!"

I took a step back from Allen. "Is that the reason why you didn't come to the hospital or his funeral?"

Allen, now crying, nodded his head. "We all had way too much to drink and got into a pretty heated argument. I don't even know how it got to that point, but it did. Johnny had enough, so he was going to leave. Sharon begged for Johnny and his girlfriend to stay. They both had too many drinks to drive. Just as Johnny was considering staying, I told him to leave. I took it a step too far when I told him to die on the way home." Allen began to sob. "I didn't mean it, Victor, I really didn't.

"Later that night, Johnny's dad called and left a message telling me he was in a bad accident, and he died. I told Sharon what happened, and she began to scream at me, telling me it was all my fault. She got dressed and left, and I haven't seen her since. How was I going to look Johnny's parents in the eye and tell them the reason why their son is dead is because of me?"

I was boiling with anger at that point and could feel it consuming me the more I looked at Allen's face. Before I knew it, I had punched him square in the jaw and watched Allen stumble backward and fall. He looked up at me and groaned, "I deserved that."

"You deserve a whole lot more than what I just gave you!" I snarled. "I will never forgive you for what you did!"

I stormed back into the sports bar leaving Allen holding his jaw and crying.

"I should have told him to stay!" Allen cried out.

I was so upset with Allen. How could he let Johnny get behind the wheel, knowing he was too drunk to drive? How could you be so angry with someone that you would wish death on him? No wonder Sharon left him. She tried to prevent Johnny from driving, and Allen pushed him out. I could only imagine how she felt when she got the news of Johnny's death. I left the sports bar and went home.

I lay in my bed, recreating the argument between Johnny and Allen. I imagined myself being there. I know I wouldn't have let it get that far. However, I wasn't there, so there was no use playing *What If*.

I fell asleep and found myself in a familiar room in my dream. Jesus was already sitting at the table. He motioned me to come and sit.

"I saw what you did to Allen," He began.

"He deserved it," I retorted. "He let Johnny die!"

"Johnny put himself in that situation," Jesus consoled. "He made the choice to drive while intoxicated. He let pride take over in the heat of the moment."

"But Allen kicked him out," I growled.

"Did Allen drive him into that truck?" Jesus asked.

"No," I sighed.

"Then who made Johnny get behind the wheel?" Jesus demanded.

"Satan did it," I snapped, still being stubborn.

Jesus stated, "Although Satan influenced him, it was still his decision to make. Remember, everyone has free will. Satan can influence you, but you still have a choice.

"Allen feels bad about what happened to Johnny. I can see his heart. He needs someone to help him get through it."

"Sharon broke up with him so she can't help him," I reasoned.

Jesus smiled at me. "I'm talking about you, Victor."

"Why would I do that?" I questioned. "He ridiculed me, and he ignored me in public."

"Because he needs ME," Jesus responded. "Get out of your personal feelings about what he did to you. If you don't help him, he's going to die and end up where Johnny is."

I was jolted awake as soon as He finished talking.

A few days went by, and I was on my way home from work. I felt bad about punching Allen that night, so I decided to call him.

"Hey, Allen, it's Victor! How are you? I'm sorry I punched you the other night. Can we talk in person later on?"

"Yeah, you can come by," Allen grumbled. "I was just thinking that I needed someone to come by."

Allen didn't sound like himself. In fact, he sounded somewhat strange.

"Is everything okay, bro?" I inquired.

"I don't know," Allen responded. "I think you should come by. I need someone to convince me why I should keep living."

Allen then hung up the phone. I tried to call him back, but he didn't answer. I quickly left my house and drove to Allen's.

I arrived at Allen's house and knocked.

"Allen!" I shouted. "Open the door, I'm here!"

I could hear Allen turning the lock on the other side of the door, and then he slowly opened it. He didn't even speak to me. He just casually walked back to his couch and sat down. I could see a whiskey bottle on the table that was nearly empty. I also noticed a revolver next to the bottle. Six bullets were placed neatly in a straight line next to Allen's gun.

"What are you doing, Allen?" I asked nervously.

"What does it look like I'm doing, genius?" Allen

sharply retorted. "I'm going to kill myself!"

"Don't do this," I pleaded.

Allen picked up his whiskey bottle and drank the last of it. "I got my friend killed, my girlfriend left me because of it, and you hate me because of it."

"I don't hate you, Allen," I pleaded. "Upset, yes, but I don't hate you! We are still friends!"

"You're not my friend!" Allen shouted. Then he picked up the gun and put the bullets in it.

"Where should I shoot myself, Vic?" Allen taunted. "Should I shoot myself here?" Allen pointed the barrel of the gun at his heart. "Or maybe I should shoot myself here." He then pointed the gun to his temple.

I was shaking and terrified. Allen was one trigger pull away from killing himself, and unfortunately, I was going be a witness to it. I had to talk him out of it and fast.

"Allen, you called me over here to convince you not to kill yourself, right?"

"Yes," Allen agreed.

"Put the gun down and let me try."

"No," Allen denied. "The gun stays in my hand. If I'm convinced, then I'll put the gun down."

I didn't know what to do or say. I was in a real situation; one I had never been in before. I was afraid if I said the wrong thing, Allen was going to pick up the gun and shoot himself. The look in his eyes was telling me that he was very serious about ending his life. His demeanor was like someone who was possessed, not drunk. I took a deep breath, and I spoke.

"Allen, remember you all ridiculed me when I told you all about the things I was going through after my visit with Jesus?"

Allen chuckled. "Yeah, we laughed you right out of my house."

"I want you to level with me," I started. "Hear me out, okay?"

Allen nodded his head with a smirk on his face.

"That day after I came home from Johnny's funeral, Jesus took me to hell to show me what it was like."

Allen began to laugh. "You really want me to pull this trigger, don't you? Continue, I need a good laugh before I leave here."

"Allen, hell is real!" I exclaimed. "If you pull that trigger and kill yourself, your body will die, but your spirit will live. Where your spirit goes depends on the decisions you make while you are alive."

"Let me guess, Jesus showed you this?" Allen asked sarcastically.

"Yes," I affirmed. I wanted to tell him that Johnny was there, but that would've upset Allen.

"I saw my great-grandfather there," I continued. "He's in torment right now because he rejected Jesus."

"So, Jesus sent your great-grandfather to hell because

he rejected Him?" Allen inquired.

"No, he sent himself there," I corrected. "Jesus died on the cross to save us from our sins. He came down here to die so we can avoid going to hell. Jesus loves you, Allen. He loves you so much that He's willing to forgive you for all the things you did. He already paid for it."

"I don't believe in Jesus, Vic," Allen flatly stated.

"Why?" I questioned.

Allen, still holding the gun, thought about it. "Because my dad didn't believe in Jesus, that's why."

"Wouldn't you want to know for yourself?" I pressed. "You are going off someone else's unbelief, Allen."

I took out my Bible and found John 3, verse 17. I read it aloud to Allen. "For God sent not his Son into the world to condemn the world, but that the world through Him might be saved."

"What does that mean?" Allen asked.

"It means Jesus was not sent here to point out your mistakes," I answered. "He was sent here to save you. I know you are feeling like you're at a dead-end right now. I'm here to tell you that Jesus can help you. Everything you are going through is temporary. If you kill yourself, you are going to regret it for eternity. Please, put the gun down, Allen. I'm begging you, bro! Let Jesus help you."

Tears began to fill Allen's eyes.

"Can this Jesus save me?"

"Of course, He can," I comforted.

"When did you commit to Him?" Allen inquired.

I leaned back in my chair to think about what Allen just asked me. Although Jesus had shown me so much over the past few months, I had not fully committed to Him. Allen had exposed something I should have done a long time ago. I leaned forward in my chair and put my head into my hands. Then I got out of the chair, and I got down on my knees. With tears flowing down my face, I choked up and answered, "Today."

Allen slowly put the gun down on the table. I took the gun and removed the bullets. Allen got on his knees with me, and I began to pray.

"God, we both come to You because we need You. Please forgive us for our sins. We commit our lives to You now. We ask You to guide us from here on out. We thank You for saving us. We turn away from our sins as we follow You. We thank You in Jesus' name, amen."

After we were finished praying, Allen got up, went to his cabinet, and removed all of his bottles of alcohol. He began to pour them all down the drain in his kitchen sink.

"Jesus really does exist, Vic!" he said excitedly. "I was drunk when you came here. I've been drinking nonstop since I woke up this morning. When we were praying, I could feel the drunkenness leave my body! I'm sober now, Vic!"

I was shocked. I looked at Allen, and he actually

appeared to be sober! Even the alcohol smell was gone!

"Allen, this is amazing!" I exclaimed. "I want you to come to church with me this Sunday."

"Okay," Allen agreed. "Vic, I'm sorry for the way I treated you."

"It's okay; I forgive you," I resolved. "I'm sorry I punched you."

"That's ok, bro," Allen forgave. "You punch like a child anyway!"

We both laughed as we walked to the door.

"Wait," Allen mentioned. He went back to get his gun and the bullets. He wrapped it in one of his towels and handed it to me. "Get rid of this for me, bro," he added. "I won't need it anymore."

I smiled. "I know exactly where to take this." I drove to the creek and tossed the gun and bullets into the water. I took a deep breath and let out a heavy sigh of relief, "Thank You, Jesus."

CHAPTER 13

ANOTHER TRIP TO HELL

****

Allen came to church with me that Sunday. He was nervous, just like I was when I first went. I introduced him to Kyle and Candace. I could tell he wasn't as nervous once we sat down. I talked Allen through the worship and told him to clear his mind, open his heart, and just talk to God.

Something really changed in me that day at Allen's house. I was fully committed to Jesus since then. I could tell that He was in my heart, and I really wanted to live for Him. I was making an effort to drink less alcohol, was spending more time in the Word, and was attending church more regularly. Allen and I grew closer in our friendship as well. He no longer felt like he was responsible for Johnny's death. He understood that Johnny made his own decision to drive drunk. Allen even came over to Kyle's house a few times for dinner. They told us they lost a son, and God gave them two in return. I finally told Allen everything Jesus showed me, even about Johnny. It was a hard pill for Allen to swallow at first, but it made him grow stronger in his walk with Jesus.

Although some time had passed since I had an encounter with Jesus, I didn't feel like He was far away. In fact, I felt as close to Him as I had ever felt. There was a strong desire to share my experience with Jesus to my mom and dad. The time was not right because I felt like I still had a lot to learn. Later that week, Jesus came to me in my dream.

"Victor, I am so pleased with what you have done over the past few months. You have helped Allen get back on his feet, you have grown in your walk with Me, and you are establishing yourself as a follower."

"Thank You, but this is all because of You," I responded.

"You still made the choices," Jesus insisted.

Jesus stretched out His hand for me to take. "Come with Me; I have more things to show you."

I knew I was going to visit hell again. I wasn't looking forward to it, but I knew I had to go. I put my hand in His, and instantly we were standing over my sleeping body in my bedroom. Jesus looked at me, looking at my body. He could tell I was feeling uneasy about seeing my body like that.

"It's okay, Victor," He assured. "Your body will be

protected while we are gone."

Jesus put His hand on my shoulder, and instantly we were in hell. When the demons saw Jesus, they scattered away in every direction.

"No demon can lay a hand on you unless I allow it," Jesus promised. Then He took me to a huge, dark mountain. "There is a prison inside the mountain," Jesus said. "We will go in and take a look."

We went inside. This place had cells just like a prison. Each cell was carved out of the mountain. I could smell the rotting flesh mixed with the sulfur. The air was so thick I could almost grab it and form it into a shape. I could hear the wails and the moans of the lost souls in this terrible place. I could also hear the demons laughing as they tormented the souls in the cells. Some of the tormented souls that saw Jesus reached out to Him, but they could not touch Him. They began to cry out, "Save me, Jesus!" one shouted.

"I believe in You now!" cried another.

"I'm sorry for all the things I did!" one shouted from a distance.

"It's too late for them," Jesus said in a somber voice. "I did all I could to show them the truth, but they rejected Me. Now they will be here for eternity, where there is no rest, and the torment is never-ending, and the fire will never be quenched."

We finally stopped at one of the cells, and Jesus

pointed at it. "Go and take a look."

I slowly walked toward the cell. There was a man sitting in the middle of the cell. He looked to be in his thirties. He was strapped to the chair with chains that appeared to have just cooled from being on fire because they had a faint red glow to it. He looked up at Jesus.

"Please stop this torment, Jesus," he said weakly.

"Peace be still," Jesus said.

Suddenly, the man seemed to be aware, and he livened up a bit.

"Who is this?" I asked.

"His name is Richard; he is your cousin," Jesus informed. "He died when you were ten years old."

Richard looked at me. "Who are you?" he inquired.

"My name is Victor Storey," I answered.

"Little Victor?" Richard questioned. "I used to call you Little Victor when your mother brought you by sometimes. My goodness, the last time I saw you, you were a little boy! You don't remember me, do you?"

I shook my head. "I don't remember you."

Richard then realized that I was standing next to Jesus and not in torment. "You should not be here, Victor. If they find you, they will do horrendous things to you!"

"It's okay, Jesus brought me here," I explained.

"You're still alive?" Richard marveled.

"Yes, I am," I affirmed.

Richard looked at Jesus and began to weep. "I failed You, Jesus. I'm here because of the many wrong choices I made when I was alive. I didn't come to You when You called me. I loved the world more than I loved You. I partied, held grudges, fornicated, and abused drugs. I'm here because I sent myself here." Richard hung his head and continued to weep bitterly. He then looked up at me.

"Don't make the same mistakes I made, or you will end up in here with me, you understand? Follow Jesus, Victor. Listen to Him. Tell everyone about this place, so no one else comes here!"

The chains began to glow red with heat, and Richard began to scream. Long worms with sharp teeth came out of the walls, and they crawled into his mouth, eyes, ears, and nose. The worms burned his skin as they crawled over his body. His screams were muffled now because of the worms crawling in his throat and mouth. Soon his entire cell erupted into flames and consumed him. The worms were unaffected by the flames, and I could still see them tormenting Richard. I turned away and began to cry. Jesus put His hand on my shoulder. "Richard was called to do mighty works for Me, but he rejected Me."

"How did he end up here?" I wondered.

A screen appeared, and I was able to see Richard's last day before he died. He was getting ready to go to a party. "It's at this time that I told him not to go to that party," Jesus pointed out.

The doorbell rang, and Richard went to answer it. It was one of his friends who was inviting him to a revival at his church later that night, but Richard turned him down.

"Had he gone with his friend to church, he would've given his life to Me on that day," Jesus added.

The time fast-forwarded to Richard being at the party. He was drinking, smoking, and dancing to the music. I saw Richard pause for a second as if he had a thought that ran across his mind.

"It was right then when I told him he should leave," Jesus mentioned.

An attractive woman came over and asked Richard to dance. He set his drink down and went to the dance floor. As soon as he turned away, a man walked by and dropped something into his drink. No one saw the man do it. When Richard came back, he picked up his glass and finished his drink. Minutes later, Richard collapsed and died. The trending drug the man put in Richard's drink had stopped his heart.

"Richard woke up in this place of torment because he died in his sins," Jesus clarified. "If he went to the revival at church with his friend, he would have given his life to Me, and he would have done wonderful things for My sake. The demons assigned to his life by Satan knew this as well, so they planned that party knowing there was a chance he would go.

Richard had free will, and he made the wrong choice with that free will. "This place was never meant for man. It was created for the fallen angels that were kicked out of Heaven. Satan is deceiving the people and they are allowing him access to do it. He promises worldly pleasures to them, things that please the flesh.

"Victor, I'm showing you these things so you can tell others about your experiences. Many people will not believe you, even in the church. Nevertheless, many will hear and believe your testimony, and you will lead them to Me. This is your destiny, Victor. You will not be alone in your journey, for I will always be with you."

"I understand," I nodded.

"It's time to go back now," Jesus directed. He took me by the hand, and we traveled out of hell at the speed of light back to my room. When we arrived, I saw an angel beside my bed! His wings were outstretched, surrounding my bed! He was protecting my soul-less body. When he saw Jesus, he kneeled. "There was an attack on him while you were gone. I fended off the attack, and all is well now."

Jesus acknowledged the angel, and then it vanished before my eyes. I looked at Jesus.

"What attack?" I questioned.

"It was a spiritual attack," Jesus explained. "Demons tried to attack your body, but I told you that you are protected."

"Thank You," I said. "I see how much You care for us."

"You really haven't seen how much I care for you," Jesus replied.

I turned to my body and re-entered it. With a gasp of air, my spirit reconnected to my body. I got out of the bed and began to worship God.

CHAPTER 14

A DIFFERENCE IN BELIEFS

****

For the next few days, I thought of ways to tell my mom and dad about the things that happened to me over the past few months. I felt like it was time to bring them together and talk to them about Jesus. I invited them both to my house on an afternoon when they both would be free. When they finally arrived, they both noticed how happy I looked.

"Victor, you must have another girlfriend," Mom teased.

"No, Mom, not at the moment," I corrected.

"I haven't seen you look this happy since I got you that race car set for your ninth birthday," Dad gleamed.

"Come in and have a seat," I motioned with a smile. "I'll tell you all why I'm so happy."

I told them about how Jesus appeared to me. I told them I was reading the Bible and that I was now saved. I also told them about Kyle and Candace and how they had been mentoring me in my walk with Jesus. I even explained to them the reason why Stacy and I were no longer together was because of my desire to follow Jesus. When I finished, my mom and dad looked at each other.

"Son, I really don't know what to say," Dad started. "I think I speak for both of us when I say we will love you no matter which religious preference you choose to follow."

"What does this have to do with us?" Mom glared.

"I know you don't believe in God, Mom," I sighed, "but He does exist, and He is very real."

My mom scowled at me. "There is no such thing as God!"

"So, are you saying everything I told you was a lie?" I challenged.

"I don't know, Victor," she concluded. "I think whatever you are going through is strictly scientific."

"Son, you said Jesus came to you in your dreams," Dad chimed in. "That's kind of hard to take in."

"How do you explain Jesus giving scriptures to me in my dreams that turned out to be real scriptures?" I retorted.

"You probably read them before," Mom snapped. "It was stored in your subconscious."

"Mom, I have never read a Bible in my life until after

Jesus spoke to me," I disputed.

I took a deep breath and sighed. "Mom, Dad, I love you two so much. I know you are not believers; this is why I am talking to you now. Even though you two don't believe in Jesus, He still paid the price for your sins and mine."

My dad rolled his eyes in disgust. "Son, please don't come at me with this church stuff."

"Dad, it's my job to let you know. Let me finish, and you can do whatever you want afterward."

I continued, "If you call out to Jesus and turn away from your sins, He will forgive you. You have to accept Jesus into your heart."

"Are you finished?" my mom asked sharply.

"Yes," I replied. "At least give it an honest try."

Mom and Dad got up and headed to the door.

"I saw Grandma Victoria, too," I added. "She spoke to me."

Dad turned around with a shocked look on his face.

"She looked just like the picture you gave me a while back," I explained, looking at my mom.

"Is that why you asked for a younger picture of her?" Mom inquired.

"Yes," I affirmed. "I even know why she spoke in that strange language on her death bed before she died."

My dad was fighting back the tears at that point. "Why is that?" he choked up.

"She knew she was surrounded by non-believers that night. She prayed in her heavenly language to God that someone in this family would be open to hearing the gospel. I was the one who was open to listening to the gospel since she passed away. Everyone else in our family line since Victoria rejected Jesus."

My dad walked toward me, saying, "Son, I didn't tell you everything that happened that night. Before Grandma passed away, she looked at me and smiled."

"I know that already, Dad," I resolved.

Dad smiled at me. "What I didn't tell you was what she said to me after she smiled at me. She pointed at me and quietly said, "Your seed." I didn't understand why she said that to me. I understand now. She meant the next person to accept the gospel would come from my seed!" My dad put both of his hands on his head in disbelief. "I believe you now."

"Are you serious right now?" my mom chided. "It doesn't make any sense!" My mom turned around and stormed out of the house. She slammed the door shut behind her.

"She'll be okay once she calms down," dad promised. "You have to admit; this is a lot to take in, especially for someone who does not think God exists. I'll give her a call later and talk to her."

Dad put his hand on my shoulder. "Son, I'm going to go home and give Jesus an honest look. I'm not guaranteeing anything, but I will search my heart and be open." He hugged me and left. I closed the door behind him, leaned back against the door, and let out a huge sigh.

CHAPTER 15

ROUND TABLE DISCUSSIONS

****

I talked to Allen about Jesus taking me to hell to see my cousin, Richard. I told him that Jesus wanted me to tell the people about my experiences.

"That's awesome!" Allen exclaimed. "I wish I could have a testimony to tell people."

"Actually, you do," I suggested. "You almost committed suicide, remember? After we prayed, you were instantly sober! You were delivered from drinking that day!"

Allen thought about what I said. "I guess you're right, bro. That was a miraculous day."

"That's right," I added. "Someday, you will help others who might be thinking about suicide and prevent them from making a huge mistake."

A faraway look came on Allen's face. "That would be something special to help others like that."

Never in a million years would I think Allen and I would be that close as friends. We hung out sometimes, but mainly because of Johnny. He was the one who introduced us. Johnny and I were best friends, but it was based on worldly interests. Allen and I are structuring our friendship through Jesus. We attend church together, we study the Bible together, and we pray together. We both had grown together in Christ. In many ways, Allen had become my brother.

Allen and I spent a lot of time studying the Bible with Kyle and Candace. We even introduced them to our round table discussions, but this time, each of our topics were scripturally related. It really kept us engaged in our learning and kept Kyle and Candace updated on their studies as well. In fact, they liked the round table discussions so much that they wanted to use it with the members of the church staff.

Sunday at church, the pastor taught from the book of Acts. He told us we were living from the book, even to this day. We were to continue what Jesus taught the disciples in our modern-day by preaching the word of God, healing the sick, and being kind to each other despite if we are treated otherwise.

I hadn't read the book of Acts yet, so I decided to read a couple of chapters to get familiar with it. One of the things I noticed was the boldness of Peter. I remember reading in the gospels where Peter had denied Jesus three times. Peter really took the things he learned from Jesus and applied it with great faith. He was bold and unashamed of Jesus. Peter exemplified being about the Father's business.

I also learned about Saul of Tarsus. He killed many Christians and had lots of them put in prison. He led a heavy persecution against the Christians until he had his own encounter with Jesus at Damascus. Jesus came to him in a bright, blinding light and asked him why he was persecuting Him. Saul was blinded for three days and was instructed to meet Ananias in Damascus. Afterward, Saul was baptized and filled with the Holy Spirit and began to teach everywhere he went.

Saul's name was later changed to Paul. He was used to do many wonderful works for God. Saul/Paul was a man who persecuted Christians, killed them, and was on a mission to destroy them. After meeting with Jesus, and with the help of Ananias, Paul led many people to Jesus and performed many miracles that his disciples performed as well. In some ways, Paul reminded me of myself: a nonbeliever in Jesus who became a believer through an encounter with Jesus, Himself. Now Jesus wants to use me to bring others to Him with my experiences. *This is awesome*, I thought. *It's like my life was being connected to the stories in the Bible!* "This should be in a book!" I exclaimed aloud.

Just months ago, I didn't want to read the Bible. I

thought it to be boring and dry. Now I'm studying scriptures and reading several chapters before I go to sleep at night. I've downloaded the Bible to my phone and listen to it while I'm at work. I felt like I was truly becoming a student of the Word.

That Sunday at church, I was taking notes during the sermon. I looked up briefly and locked eyes with the prettiest woman I had ever seen. I nodded and gave her a quick wave. She responded with a smile and a wave of her own and then returned her attention to the pastor. I sighed and continued with my notetaking. After church ended, I saw the woman in the lobby. I wanted to talk to her, but I was nervous, so I quickly turned around. Quite some time had passed since Stacy and I had broken up. That relationship was not built on a solid foundation.

Nevertheless, I was never attracted to a woman in the church before. How would I approach her? I definitely was not going to use a cheesy pick-up line. Suddenly, I felt a tap on my shoulder. I turned around, and there she was standing in front of me.

"Hi," she smiled.

"Hi, how are you?" I greeted nervously.

"I'm Victoria," she announced with a warm smile.

"Seriously, your name is Victoria?" I marveled.

"Yes, it is," Victoria affirmed. "My friends call me Vicky for short."

"My name is Victor!" I returned.

"Get out of here!" Victoria exclaimed. "What are the odds?"

"My great-grandmother was named Victoria also!" I added.

"Some ice breaker, huh?" Victoria commented.

I nodded. "Hey, would you like to get something to eat sometime?"

"Sure," Victoria agreed.

We traded phone numbers, and then I went home. Shortly after I got home, Victoria sent me a text.

"Hi Victor, it was a pleasure to meet you. I just wanted to let you know that I really enjoyed talking with you today. I look forward to meeting up with you for lunch. Take care!"

I responded, "It was nice talking with you, too. I'm glad we got to connect today."

I was surprised she texted me so soon, but I was glad she did. Although I was attracted to Vicky, I wanted to be her friend first. That was not the case with Stacy, as it was strictly physical, and then we became friends.

Later that week, I was at Kyle's house. We all were having our round table discussion. After we finished, Allen gave me a nudge. I looked at him, and he was wearing this huge, cheesy grin.

"I saw you talking to her on Sunday," he teased.

Kyle and Candace were beaming at me.

"Yeah, we talked," I clarified, "but, we're just friends!

That's where we are beginning at."

"Well, Vicky is a very nice person," Candace added. "I think you two look really good together. Just enjoy the friendship and let it build from there."

"Yes, ma'am," I concurred.

"I believe you two will be very good friends for a long time," Kyle assured.

***

As we were leaving, Allen approached me. "Vic, how did you deal with us when we were ridiculing you when you first started this?"

"Well, for starters, I saw how Christians reacted after I used to ridicule them," I began. "They were always peaceful, and no one ever got angry at me, despite my harshness at times. Jesus told His disciples that they were going to be persecuted for His namesake, but to know that they persecuted Him first."

"Well, I guess I'm on the right path," Allen mumbled. "I told my parents and my brother, and they didn't take it too well."

"Yeah, I know how that can be," I consoled. "I wasn't fully committed to Christ yet, and you all laughed me out of your house."

"Yeah, I know," Allen remarked regretfully. "Now the shoe is on my foot, and I don't know how I can deal with this."

"I look at it as an honor," I explained. "We are going

through some of the same things Jesus and His disciples went through."

"I guess you are right," Allen understood. "My brother won't even hang out with me now; he barely speaks to me. He thinks I'm going to snitch him out or something."

I chuckled. "Remember when someone came to Jesus and they told Him that his mother and brothers were outside waiting for Him?"

"Yeah, I remember," Allen replied.

"He said that His family were those who do the will of His Father. Not exactly in those words, but you know what I mean."

"My mother was upset about my decision as well," I added. "I love my mom and dad, but at the end of the day, you, Kyle, and Candace are my family."

"Right now, you all are the only ones I got," Allen concluded.

"Don't forget about Jesus," I proposed. "He understands what you are going through. One day, they will come around, but for now, what we can do is pray for them."

CHAPTER 16

THE ATTACK

****

Vicky and I finally met up for our lunch date. I was so nervous. I wanted everything to be perfect. I made sure my hair was trimmed and neat, I wore my best casual outfit, and I took some extra mints so my breath would be pleasant after our meal. When Vicky showed up, I could see that she commanded attention. It was not in a narcissistic way, but in a respectful way. She wasn't even wearing makeup. She had a natural beauty that shined. Makeup would not have done her any justice. Her face had a soft glow that brightened my day when I looked at her.

She came over, and we ordered our food. We talked while we waited. Vicky was very good at holding a conversation. We discussed sports, our hometowns, our favorite foods, and how we became Christians. I was nervous about telling her my story, but when I was done telling her about it, I saw that she easily believed it. She used to listen to people's testimonies about having encounters with Jesus and being taken to hell. She also read books about people who had near-death experiences. After listening to her talk about that, I felt more comfortable sharing with her.

Vicky and I also spent time laughing at random things we did as kids. I told her about the time I fell off the ladder, climbing it after my dad specifically told me to stay off of it. I got hurt and tried to hide it, but he knew because he was spying on me the whole time. Vicky told me that when she was playing in the bathroom, she placed the entire roll of toilet paper in the toilet, and after she flushed, the toilet overflowed. We had a natural enjoyment of each other's company.

Over the course of a few weeks, Vicky and I had lunch three times. We also texted occasionally to check up on each other. One thing I admire about Vicky is her genuine love for Jesus. She seems to spend more time with Him than her friends. She knows who she is in Christ, something I'm still figuring out.

One night, after talking on the phone with Vicky, I decided to turn in early for the night. I had a long day at work, and I wanted to get a few extra hours of rest. I was only asleep a couple of hours when I was awakened by a loud thump that came from my living room. I got out of my bed to investigate and gave myself a pinch to my arm to make sure I was not

dreaming, then I slowly walked towards my living room. I heard the thump again, only it was much louder this time. It felt like the entire house shook.

I made it to my living room and flipped the switch to turn on the lights. The lights didn't come on, and I was getting nervous. I heard the loud thump again. I noticed that the living room was much darker than normal, even with the lights off. I could actually feel the dark. This was all too familiar for me. Suddenly, I saw a silhouette standing by my door. It looked like my mother. She's the only person who has the keys to my house other than me. She has never come to my house, unannounced.

"Mom, is that you?" I questioned in a shaky voice.

No response; the figure just stood there very still.

"Mom," I called out again. "This is not funny; what are you doing here this late?"

The silhouette slowly moved towards me, and then in a blink of an eye, the silhouette was right in front of my face! It quickly put its hands around my neck and began to squeeze! I could see that this thing looked like my mother, but I knew it wasn't. This was a demonic force attacking me!

"You belong to us, Victor!" it threatened in a low, growling voice.

I could hardly breathe as the demon's hands clutched tighter around my neck. I mustered up just enough strength to say one word, "Jesus!" The demon let me go and covered its ears. When I saw how the demon was reacting, I began to say Jesus' name repeatedly.

"Get out of my house in the name of Jesus!" I shouted.

The demonic creature, now on all fours in an unnatural position and still looking like my mother, began to retreat through the door!

As soon as it left, my lights came on. I ran to my room, grabbed my Bible, and began to pray. When I was done, I called out to Jesus.

"Why did this demon attack me?" I asked aloud.

I waited a few minutes, but there was no answer. I wasn't disappointed because I knew better now. Jesus will answer me when the time is right. I was just happy that demonic presence was gone!

I finally fell asleep and later found myself in that familiar room. Jesus walked in and sat down. "Why did that demon attack me?" I questioned.

"Satan has become aware," Jesus started. "He knows you have been following Me. He wants to bring you back because he knows who you are destined to be. He will do whatever it takes to keep you from reaching that."

"How come You didn't help me?" I probed. "That demon was attacking me, and I called out to You."

"I did," Jesus defended plainly.

A confused look came over my face. Jesus smiled at me. "What did the demon do when you called My name?"

My jaw dropped. "It let me go and ran away!" I answered excitedly.

"You used My name, and you had faith behind it," Jesus explained. "That evil spirit had to leave because you used your authority in Me. Sadly, many of My more experienced followers do not use their authority, or they don't know how to use it. Many of My people don't call on Me when they go through tough times. I don't want them to go through some of the trials they endure. In many cases, they blame My Father instead of calling on Him."

Jesus smiled at me and put His hand on my shoulder. "You called on Me like a child calls out to his dad when he needs him. I am Your Father, Victor. Do not hesitate to call out to Me like a child. I will protect you. I will never leave you, even when you think I am not there, I am there."

Jesus started to walk to the door.

"That's it?" I pressed. "We're done?"

"Yes, we are," Jesus affirmed. "You don't want to be late for work now, do you?"

I awoke after He spoke this. About five seconds later, my alarm started to sound off. I got out of bed and got ready to go to work. I was thinking about what Jesus told me about Satan. I had his attention now. When I was just living my life in sin, he wasn't worried about me. He knew at that time I was on my way to eternal death. Now he saw that I had turned my attention to Jesus. Satan was angered at that, and now he saw me as a potential threat to his plans. This made me excited. I wanted to see what Jesus had in store for me. I was also nervous. I knew Satan would not hold back on his attacks on me as well. I knew in order for me to be prepared for his attacks, I would have to read the Bible more, learn to pray against Satan's attacks, and surround myself with people who will pray with me and for me. Most importantly, I had a growing relationship with Jesus Christ, and from what I know, He already defeated Satan when He rose from the grave.

CHAPTER 17

GROWTH

****

Vicky and I have been seeing more of each other over the past few weeks. We're still only good friends, and we're totally fine with that. She started coming over to Kyle's house with the rest of us to participate in our round table discussions. We were talking and texting more, too. We were now sitting next to each other in church.

Allen is flourishing in the church. He's grown much closer to God in recent weeks. He's planning on going on a mission trip sometime next year to help with those who are less fortunate. He also spends a lot of his spare time talking to those with alcohol problems, and he shares his testimony with teens of how he overcame his suicidal thoughts.

Kyle and Candace lead the round table discussions with

the church staff and leaders. Along with the lead pastors, they make sure the staff knows what they are here for: to educate the congregation on the repentance of sin, to serve God, and to prepare the church to be the Light that Jesus wants us to be.

Things have been going very smoothly lately, but in the back of my mind, I knew Jesus was going to take me to hell one more time. I really was not looking forward to it, but I knew it was going to happen. I had to prepare myself mentally for it.

I was relaxing on my couch watching TV when I heard a knock on my door. To my surprise, it was Stacy! I opened the door.

"What are you doing here?" I asked.

Stacy was dressed very provocatively and was wearing more makeup than usual. She walked in and sat down. I came over and sat down on the far side of the couch.

"Sorry I came over unannounced," she began. "How have you been?"

"Fine," I commented.

Stacy got up and sat closer to me. "I really missed you, Vic," she started. "I'm sorry about everything."

"Me too, but ..."

Stacy cut me off. "I want things to go back to the way they were, don't you?"

I was looking into Stacy's eyes. I suddenly realized I

wasn't over her like I thought I was. I did miss her. I began to reminisce about our time together, our dates, the parties, our laughs together ... I was losing myself in her eyes. I began to hear a faint voice in my mind. I couldn't understand what it was saying because it was too faint to hear. Then I heard another voice. It was much louder and clearer.

"Kiss her," it urged. "Just kiss her one time, it won't hurt."

Now several voices were speaking to me at the same time, and they were all telling me to kiss Stacy. However, that small, faint voice was telling me something different, but I could not understand what it was saying.

Stacy moved in to kiss me. Everything was going in slow motion. The voices in my head were screaming at me to kiss her now. Amazingly, I could still hear the faint voice but still couldn't make out what it was saying. Then I began to think about Vicky and how much I really cared about her. I thought about all we were building together. It would all go to waste if I kissed Stacy. Now I could understand what the faint voice was saying.

"You are being tempted, flee!"

I quickly snapped out of my daze and placed my hands on Stacy's shoulders. I gently pushed her back. "I can't do this, Stacy," I contended with a sigh. I was irritated now. "Do you really think you can just come back here months later and just have everything go back to *normal*?"

I got up, walked to the door, and opened it. Stacy stood up and looked at me with a shocked look on her face.

"You're kicking me out?" she marveled.

"I'm seeing someone else," I explained. "Our time together is over."

"If I leave out this time, Vic, I'm not coming back."

I nodded. Stacy stormed out, and I closed the door behind her. After I closed the door, I put my back against it and slowly sank down until I was crouched on the floor. I breathed a sigh of relief. I was annoyed at Stacy's boldness to come back months later to try to tempt me as if I were sitting at home waiting for her to come back.

After stewing in my anger for little bit, I finally went to bed for the night. The next thing I knew, I was in the "dream room" waiting for Jesus to enter. I sat there for about five minutes, and then He finally arrived. He sat across from me and let out a sigh.

"You resisted temptation," He observed, "but you were directing your anger and rejection at the wrong person."

"What do You mean?" I inquired. "The only people in the house were Stacy and me."

"Ephesians 6:12," Jesus expounded. "We wrestle not against flesh and blood, but against principalities, powers, rulers of the darkness of this world, and spiritual wickedness in high places."

"What does that mean?" I pressed.

"Do you remember your vision at the movie theater where you saw all the demons?" Jesus reminded.

"Yes, I do," I answered.

"Things happen in the spirit realm first before they manifest in the natural," Jesus explained.

I was confused about what Jesus was explaining to me.

"So, you're saying what Stacy was trying to do was spiritual?" I questioned.

Jesus continued, "There were spirits behind her actions to tempt you and draw you into fornication. Satan tried to intimidate you when that demonic spirit attacked you in your living room. That didn't work, so he tried to tempt you with a lustful spirit. You were focused on Stacy, not the spirits influencing her intentions."

"What were those voices in my head telling me to kiss her?" I asked.

"That was your flesh," Jesus clarified.

"I heard another voice," I went on. "Although it was a faint voice, I could still hear it."

Jesus simplified, "That was your spirit. It knows what is right, but your flesh usually wants to do things that are not right but feel good. It's a constant battle, and sometimes, the flesh wins. The more you read My Word and draw closer to Me, the stronger your spirit will be. Fasting helps to strengthen your spirit while at the same time weakening your fleshly desires. Satan tried to tempt Me when I walked the earth."

"Yes, I read about that in the Bible," I concurred.

"I want you to read Ephesians 6:12-18," Jesus said. "Thirteen through eighteen will explain how to arm yourself against spiritual attacks with spiritual armor. In the future, you will look past the person and see what's influencing them to act the way they act."

As soon as Jesus finished talking, I immediately woke up. Later that day, I did what Jesus told me to do, and I read Ephesians 6:12-18. I learned I had a spiritual armor that I was to wear. I had a belt of truth, a breastplate of righteousness, shoes of the gospel of peace, a shield of faith, a helmet of salvation, and a sword of the spirit. I suddenly realized how strategic Satan was. Although I thought I was over Stacy, deep down, I still had feelings for her. Satan knew this, and he used it against me. If I had my spiritual armor on, I would've dealt with that situation completely differently.

I couldn't wait to tell Allen about my latest encounter with Jesus. Not only was I excited about learning about my newfound armor, but I was also excited because I had taken my next step in my walk of faith.

CHAPTER 18

A SPIRITUAL ENCOUNTER

****

Sunday morning arrived, and I was getting dressed for church. My dad called me on the phone.

"Son, how are you?"

"I'm fine, dad," I responded. "What's up?"

"I'm on my way to your house," dad started. "I really have to talk to you."

"I'm about to leave out for church," I explained. "Can't this wait until later?"

"I'm afraid not, Son," he urged. "I really have to talk to you in person. I'm not that far from your house, and I will only take a few minutes of your time."

"Okay, dad."

Dad arrived shortly after his call, and he was now

sitting on my couch wearing a nervous smile on his face and anxiously rubbing his hands.

"What's on your mind, dad?" I pressed.

"Son, I told you that I was going to take an honest approach to Jesus. The other night, while I was in bed, I asked Jesus to show Himself to me. Nothing happened. Disappointed, I went to sleep. I dreamed I was at Grandma Victoria's deathbed. This time I was by myself. The rest of my family was not there. Grandma was sitting up in the bed, smiling at me! She spoke to me, son!"

"What did she say?" I asked excitedly.

"She told me she loved me," dad continued. "She also told me that Jesus had answered her prayers, and I should listen to her great-grandson. Victor, she told me to listen to you! I have to be honest with you, Vic. I did not believe the things you said to your mother and me. Your great-grandmother told me I should believe you! She told me this in my dream, Vic! The dream felt so real! I could see her so clearly. I woke up and realized I was wrong not to believe you. Son, I'm ready to believe now."

I could tell that my excitement was showing all over my face. I got up and gave dad a big hug. My dad gave his life to Jesus right in my living room. He came to church with me right after that. We got there about twenty minutes late, but it was well worth it. I introduced my dad to Kyle and Candace.

After church, we all went to get something to eat. Allen

and Vicky came with us. We all talked about our first encounter with Jesus. Kyle talked about his story about being robbed at gunpoint and later being shot. Allen talked about our moment when he nearly committed suicide. Candace and Vicky grew up in church, so it was an easy decision to make for them to commit to Jesus. Everyone at the table all agreed that my encounter was the most intriguing. They all have had encounters with Jesus, but only I have had a face to face encounter with Him.

After lunch, we all went home. I took my dad back to my place.

"I'm proud of the man you have become," dad concluded.

"Thanks, dad," I stated. "It appears I have a lot more to do in this life. Jesus told me what I'm to do when He is finished showing me everything."

"Your story will touch a lot of people that don't know Jesus," dad corroborated. "I'm touched just by what you have told me. I'm at a loss for words."

Dad got up to get ready to leave. "I'm going to go to the bookstore to get a Bible."

"I'm proud of you, dad," I gleamed.

"Thank you for opening up my eyes, son," dad expressed.

He gave me a hug, and then he left.

After dad left, my attention turned to my mother. We

really haven't talked that much since I told her about Jesus. When we did speak, she was somewhat short with her conversations. It almost seemed as if she was distancing herself from me. She already told me that she didn't want me preaching a sermon to her. I wondered how she would react once she finds out dad got saved. I smiled at the thought. Ultimately, it's her choice to come to Christ. I just want to make sure that if she comes around, that I'm there and ready to help her on her journey.

The next week during church service, Kyle leaned over and asked Allen and me if we wanted to be baptized. Neither of us really understood the act of being baptized, so we both sort of gave a shrug. Kyle quickly flipped through his Bible and found Mark 1:4. "John the Baptist preached the repentance and remission of sins and baptized with water." Then he turned to Acts 8:27. "The Lord led Philip to a man of Ethiopia who had come to Jerusalem to worship."

Kyle explained further, "Philip preached Jesus to him, and while they were on their way, they came across a body of water. Phillip told him if he believed with all his heart that Jesus was the Son of God, he should be baptized. That man got baptized right then and there."

Allen and I looked at each other. "I believe Jesus is the Son of God," he commented to me.

"Me too," I agreed.

"So, are you going to get baptized?" Kyle probed.

Both of us nodded.

"This is a big deal," Kyle exclaimed. "You are letting people know that you are burying the old person by going into the water. When you come out of the water, you are coming out as a new person in Christ. When Jesus died, and they put Him into that tomb, all of our sins were taken with Him. When He rose three days later, all of our sins were left behind."

Kyle told us the church would be baptizing people next Sunday. He was going to add our names to the list. Later that night, I skimmed through a few of the scriptures about baptisms. After some praying, I called Allen to see what his thoughts were. He was excited about the baptism. He was also a little nervous. Overall, both of us knew that this was a necessity.

The following Sunday after service, Allen and I got baptized. Allen went first. After he came out of the water, he raised both of his hands into the air and began to praise God. Then it was my turn. I got into the pool, and the pastor spoke to me. "I baptize you in the name of Jesus Christ." He submerged me into the pool.

When I came up, this weird feeling came over me. My mouth opened up, and I began to spew out words that I didn't understand! The words came out so smoothly. This feeling of joy overcame my entire body! It was like a shot of adrenaline. The pastor began to speak in a weird language with me, as well. Then many of the members in the church began to speak in many different languages! It was definitely one of the most bizarre moments I had ever experienced.

I asked Kyle about all that was going on after the baptism. He told me I was speaking in a heavenly language called *tongues*. He told me I was baptized in the Holy Spirit, which allowed me to communicate with God on a spiritual level. He told me he's never witnessed anyone being filled with the Holy Spirit right after they came up from the water.

I had only briefly read about the Holy Spirit a few times since I've been reading the Bible. I skimmed over it, not really understanding it. Now I found myself baptized in it. Allen was so inspired about what happened to me. He prayed later that night for the Holy Spirit to fill him while at home, and he later received it. He called me to tell me the news.

"Vic, guess what?" he began.

Allen began to speak in tongues over the phone.

"Wow, you got the Holy Spirit, too!" I yelled. "That's wonderful!"

"I just asked God to let me speak in tongues," Allen explained. "I asked, and I received."

I was so excited for Allen, and I was relieved as well. I didn't want to be the only one between us to witness this gift of the Holy Spirit. This was another chapter of my spiritual walk that was completed. I was more than excited to see what was ahead.

CHAPTER 19

MY FINAL VISIT TO HELL

****

I had one more visit to hell, and I was not looking forward to it. I had a strange feeling that this night was the night for that visit. That strange feeling proved true as Jesus showed up again to meet me.

"Victor, it's time for your final visit to hell," He proclaimed. Jesus stretched out His hand toward me. "Come with Me," He invited.

I closed my eyes, and my spirit came out of my body. I was nervous, but as soon as I touched Jesus' hand, it all went away. We traveled to hell but not as fast as the time before.

"I am very pleased with you, Victor," Jesus began. "You have been studying My Word, you have constantly been praying, and you have taken great strides to live a holy life. However, there is one more thing you will have to do, and when the time is right, you will know exactly what it is."

Right after He finished speaking, we arrived at the gates of hell. Jesus pointed to an area a great distance away. I looked and saw what appeared to be a clouded waterfall descending from the dark sky. The clouded waterfall was coming from a dimly lit opening. I looked at Jesus. I could see tears streaming down His cheeks.

"Why is that cloudy waterfall falling from the sky?" I asked.

"It's not water," Jesus wept. "Those are the lost souls that have just died on earth."

Jesus took me closer to get a better look. There were so many souls descending to this terrible place at an alarming rate.

"When will this stop?" I pondered.

"It won't stop," Jesus said plainly. "People die every second in the world. More people die without Me than with Me. Every single soul that comes here has rejected Me. Their punishment is just. I am greatly saddened that they've come here to a place that was never meant for them."

Jesus and I began to walk. I could hear the agonizing screams from the people who just arrived at this place. We stopped at an empty cell.

"Watch," Jesus pointed out. A few seconds later, a woman slammed to the cell floor. She got up and looked around. She appeared to be confused and disoriented. The woman was dressed in a business suit.

"This woman just died a minute ago," Jesus explained. "She was a lawyer who made her way to the top by being dishonest. She lied and she cheated just to become successful. I sent many of My people to talk to her about what I could do for her, but she rejected Me."

Jesus stretched out His hand and a flat-like screen appeared before me. Her life was being shown to me. I saw how she deceived and manipulated others so she could make her way to the top. I also saw the people Jesus sent to her to help her change her deceitful ways. She ignored all of them. Success meant more to her than Jesus. Jesus also showed me how she lived her life. She spread rumors with her friends about her clients, she looked down on the less fortunate, and she abused her authority as a lawyer. The worst thing about her was that she did not believe Jesus existed.

"Despite all of her sins - and there were many - I would've forgiven her if she had only repented," Jesus continued. "All she had to do was come to Me. She did not believe, and now she has died in her sins."

I turned my focus back to the woman. She was looking around, trying to find a way out. Suddenly, three demons quickly approached her, but they concealed their appearance to her. To her, they looked like three normal people.

"Where am I?" she demanded. "How did I get here?"

"You don't know where you're at?" one of the demons

taunted.

"No," the woman hissed. "How do I get out of here?"

The demons continued to play along with their masquerade conversing with the woman for several minutes, pretending to be stuck in the cell with her.

"I have a confession to make," one of the demons began. "We are the ones who led you here! My name is Greed, this is Gossip, and that is Anti-Christ!"

"Why is your name Anti-Christ?" the woman pressed. "Christ doesn't exist for you to be against Him!"

The demons began to laugh. "You stupid human," Anti-Christ snapped. "He DOES exist, and we led you away from Him!"

The demons revealed themselves to the woman, and they began to torment her. Her screams could be heard throughout the halls.

"Jesus, help me!" she screamed. "I believe in You now! I'm sorry!"

I began to cry. "How did she die?" I stammered.

"She was talking on her phone," Jesus explained. "She was not paying attention and walked into the street. She didn't have the light to cross. She was struck by a car and died instantly." Jesus turned away from the woman's cell. "Come, I have more to show you."

As we walked, the demons that saw Jesus trembled and scurried away. Now, understand, some of these demons stood over fifteen feet tall and were menacing at first sight. However, when they saw Jesus, they ran from Him. Jesus knew my thoughts and He spoke to me, "They flee from Me because I am God. The world does not believe in Me because they do not want Me to exist. They want to do what makes them happy. If I didn't exist, then they never would have been created, for I am God. The spirits that influence the world to not believe in Me are the very ones that tremble before Me. I want you to tell the people this, Victor."

"I will," I replied.

We stopped at another cell, and Jesus pointed to it. "Look in the cell," He directed.

The cell was so dark. The darkness had life to it. I could feel the evil presence the closer I walked toward it. Then I heard a voice coming from the dark cell. "Somebody help me," it said.

As I peered into the dark cell, I could now see that it was Johnny! His body was still battered from the car accident from months before. I could see that demon that was behind him at the diner when Johnny snapped at me that day. Huge, long, ugly worms crawled all over his body. They bore into his open sores and into his mouth.

Jesus stretched out His hand, and the cell became bright. The demon saw Jesus, hissed at Him, and retreated from the cell. Jesus then looked at Johnny. "Peace be still," He decreed.

Johnny now realized I was there. "Victor! What are you doing here?" Johnny questioned me.

I could barely contain myself. I had so many emotions running through me at once.

"Johnny, why didn't you listen to me?" I drilled. "Jesus died for you to keep you from this place. All you had to do was accept Him."

"Jesus is the One who sent me here!" Johnny complained while pointing at Jesus.

"No, He didn't," I retorted. "You sent yourself here. You didn't want anything to do with Jesus."

"Shut up, Vic!" Johnny shouted. "I hate you, and I hate Jesus! If you're not here to get me out, then leave!"

I looked at Jesus, and I could see His eyes welling up with tears. "It's time to go now," He said to me.

As we walked away, the demon came back to torture Johnny.

"The anti-Christ spirit has him blind," Jesus explained. "Even in this place of torment."

"I want to go home," I pleaded. "I can't take this place anymore."

"You have to experience this place in order for you to share your testimony," Jesus explained.

"Haven't I experienced enough already?" I challenged.

"I must leave you here for a little while," Jesus mentioned. "Only then you will have this testimony in your heart to tell it the way it's supposed to be told."

Jesus instantly vanished before my eyes! Suddenly, I didn't feel protected. When Jesus left, His illuminating light left with Him. I was all alone in this dark, smelly place.

"JESUS, WHERE ARE YOU?" I shouted.

I then heard a low growling voice, "He is not here!"

I began to run, but my feet became stuck in a mud-like substance. Then demons from all around began to grab and pull me in all directions. The pain I felt was beyond measure. The demons laughed and ridiculed me as they carried me away. They threw me into a dark, smelly cell. I sat in there for what seemed like hours. My hunger was so extreme that it caused me to double over in a heap of pain. My mouth was so dry from the thirst for water that my lips began to crack. My tongue was sticking to the roof of my mouth. There wasn't an ounce of moisture in the air.

All of a sudden, two demons came into my cell and dragged me out. I tried to free myself, but they were too strong. I was like a rag doll to them because of their superhuman strength. They took me to a giant pot that was filled with boiling acid. The demons strapped me down on the ground. One of the demons took some of the boiling acid and slowly poured it on my leg. I cannot begin to tell you the immense pain I was experiencing as the boiling acid ate away at my leg. The pain was so intense, I wanted to die, but I couldn't. I realized that the spirit lives forever. The body is the only thing that can die. I looked at what was left of my leg. The demons began to laugh at me. I began to hear something like dried leaves rustling. I looked at my dissolved leg, and it was beginning to heal again! Within seconds, my leg was completely restored!

"Where is your Savior?" one of the demons snarled. "You're going to be here forever!" He took out a bucket and poured worms on me.

These were not regular worms. They had sharp, razor-like teeth. They had dozens of tiny legs and were about a foot long. They had black, dingy bodies and they were squealing. I could feel every single worm crawling on me! They went into my mouth, my ears, and into my nostrils. I could feel the worms crawling inside my entire body as I lay helpless on the ground. I tried to call out to Jesus again, but I couldn't because the worms were still crawling in my mouth. The demons were laughing at me and taunting me. "Your God cannot save you from here!" they said.

The deepest feeling of despair came over me. I was being consumed in my own doubts. I was slowly drifting away into utter hopelessness. There is no hope in hell, no joy, no optimism, no peace, no grace, and no mercy. I heard people say there's a party in hell and they can't wait to go. Let me tell you something, the demons tormenting the lost souls are the only ones having fun; however, their time is running short.

There is absolutely no mercy from the demons in this

place. There is no food, no water, and no rest in hell. The demons were clawing my flesh off of me, the worms were probing my body, my skin was constantly being burned by fire, and my mind was consumed in complete despair.... all at the same time!

Suddenly, a light shown from above and the demons began to scatter away. I could move now, so I reached up, and the light began to pick me up. Jesus had come back to get me! All I could see was His hand. Once I grabbed His hand, all of my despair instantly went away. Pure elation filled my body as I ascended out of hell. I could see the worms falling off me. Within a few seconds, I was back in my room. Jesus was standing in front of me.

"Now, you have experienced hell in your heart," He stated. Jesus showed me His hands. I could see the holes in them. I looked down at His feet and could see the nail piercing holes in them as well. "I went through this so you would not go to that place," Jesus informed. He then pointed to my lifeless body still lying in the bed. Slowly, I walked over and reentered it. With a gasp of fresh air, I awoke. Jesus had already left. I jumped out of my bed and began to pray and worship Him.

CHAPTER 20

A VISIT TO HEAVEN

****

I lay sick in my bed for the next several days. This sickness was unlike any sickness I ever had. I could feel this sickness deep in my soul.

My mind was still processing my latest experience of hell. My body was still recovering from the physical part of it. My muscles felt as though I had been beaten up. I even had bruises on my body. I took a leave of absence from my job just so I could recover. Kyle and Candace brought food for me to eat. Allen came by after work to keep me company. My mom stopped by to bring her famous Chicken Noodle soup from scratch. Even Vicky paid me a visit to check on me. She baked me a Red Velvet cake with cream cheese frosting. She told me I could not eat it until I was better. As soon as she left, I ran my finger across the cake and ate some of the icing!

As I lay in my bed, I thought about how helpless I was in hell without Jesus next to me. I thought about the people in torment right now. I experienced what some of them went through. The only difference was they are still there, and they can't get out, and I was only there for a short time.

My dad stopped by and I told him about my last visit to hell. As I was speaking to him, I noticed how passionate and desperate I sounded. I finally realized what Jesus had said to me when He told me that it was in my heart now. I truly did not want anyone to go to hell, because I had lived it. It was now my mission to talk to others about my experiences. I didn't care if people believed me or not. I saw relatives and my best friend there. All I was required to do was to share my testimony and leave it for the people to decide. After all, we have free will to choose.

As much as I dreaded going to hell that last time, I had a level of optimism about the special place Jesus said He was taking me to. Could it be heaven? That was my only guess because there was no other special place, in my opinion.

Jesus came to me about a week later. It wasn't in my dream as usual. A bright light appeared by the wall in front of my bed. I got up and walked toward the light. Jesus then appeared and told me to stop. "Before you come with Me, you have to be properly dressed."

Suddenly, I was completely clothed in white. Not as white as Jesus' garments, but whiter than any other white I had ever seen. Jesus reached out His hand. "Come and see the things I have prepared for My people."

"Are we going to heaven?" I asked.

Jesus smiled at me. "Yes, we are," He affirmed.

I eagerly placed my hand in His, and in an instant, we were standing in front of the pearly gates of Heaven. The pearls that lined the golden gates were breathtakingly beautiful. The gold looked almost clear, not like the gold on earth. I could actually see through this gold.

"This is where I want My people to go," Jesus mentioned to me.

We were instantly transported to a huge park ... or garden. Maybe it was both, because I saw people eating exotic fruits from trees that I've never seen before, and they were dancing and singing. Everyone was young here. It seemed like everyone was twenty-five years and younger in heaven. Jesus read my thoughts and spoke to me. "There are no elderly here, Victor. Everyone will be young in heaven. There is no sadness, no sickness, and no worries. It's just pure happiness here."

Jesus pointed to two young men walking in the distance.

"Who are they?" I inquired.

"It's Steven and Paul," Jesus clarified.

I was shocked. In the book of Acts, Paul was there when they stoned Steven. He was Saul before his name was changed to Paul. After they stoned Steven, they tossed their garments at Paul's feet. It was an act of consenting to Steven's death. That was the beginning of the great persecution of the Christians. Now I'm looking at them walking together without a care in the world.

I could hear beautiful singing coming from every direction as we walked. Even the flowers were singing praises as we walked by. I looked down and could see that the street we were walking on was pure gold! It was the same clear gold I saw at the pearly gates. To my left, I saw a lion and a gazelle walking together. "No way!" I exclaimed.

"The predators on earth are not predators in heaven," Jesus explained.

Jesus took me to the mansions. These mansions were unlike any mansions on earth. Some were made of pure crystal, others were made with solid gold, and some were even made with precious jewels. Some mansions were still under construction. Before I could ask why, Jesus answered me. "The unfinished mansions are for My people who are still serving Me on earth. They still have many things to accomplish for Me before they come here."

"Do I have a mansion, Jesus?" I asked.

"Your foundation is being built right now," Jesus replied. "The good works you do for My namesake will contribute to the building of your mansion. You have only just begun to do My will, but in time, if you continue to walk the straight and narrow path, and finish your race, your mansion will be completed. This is why I say to build your treasures here rather than in the world. It's okay to have wealth, but don't let that be the first thing in your life. Strive to do My will, and all that you need will be given unto you."

Jesus then took me to a building that was huge in appearance. No architect in the world could build something like this. This building was elegant in design, and it was made from pure crystal. The outside was so beautiful; I could only imagine what the inside looked like. "This is where the great banquet will be held," Jesus described. "My people will dine with Me, and there will be a great celebration."

We went inside and I saw a table made of pearl. The table stretched as long as I could see. Each designated place had a chair made from a soft material I have never felt or seen before. On the back of each chair, there were names that I could not pronounce. The names were written in pure gold. The silverware, the plates, and the cups were all made of pure gold. The finest cloths draped over the entire table. A chandelier that was as long as I could see hung over the table. To say this place was supremely elegant would be a supreme understatement on so many different levels.

Jesus looked around the room with sheer admiration. "Everyone who comes here will have their own seat at the table," Jesus gleamed. "We will all sup together as a family."

We left the banquet room, and Jesus took me to a great body of water. As we walked along it, fish jumped out, praising

Jesus. The birds that flew by were singing songs of praise to Him. The water was as blue as the bluest blue, yet I could see all the way down into it. The sky was clear; no clouds could be seen anywhere. A gentle breeze made the singing flowers sway back and forth. The colors of the flowers were not earthly colors. In fact, the flowers themselves were not earthly flowers. I couldn't explain the beauty of everything around me, even if I could paint it. It was so breathtaking that I found myself welling up with tears of joy.

"Am I the only one You have done this for?" I asked.

"No," Jesus clarified. "There have been others that have shared this experience. If I had not come to those like this, then they would have all perished in hell."

"I was really that far gone?" I asked in amazement.

Jesus nodded. "Everyone receives in different ways. For some, it takes someone telling them about Me, and they receive Me right away. Others may receive Me, but they become led away because of the lusts of their fleshly desires, such as money, drugs, or sexual immorality. Some of them will experience a hardship that will eventually lead them to Me. I would rather them come to Me and stay, but better late than never."

I noticed as we walked that my feet didn't get tired. Jesus knew my thoughts and spoke, "You will not be tired here because I have taken away all weariness, all pain, all sorrow, and all your burdens I have taken away."

Jesus then began to walk on the water. After He walked a few feet, He stopped and looked back at me. "Come," He beckoned. I was hesitant to come to Him. I didn't want to fall into the water.

"My child, I would not tell you to come if I knew you would fall into the water. Trust in My ability to do the unnatural."

I took my first step, then my second step. The water was gently splashing around my feet and legs, but I didn't get wet! Even though the water was moving under my feet, it felt as if I was walking on the ground! "This is awesome!" I shouted.

"Peter asked to come out to the water with Me," Jesus shared. "He comes out and takes a few steps, and then he begins to doubt, and then he falls in. Now, he's asking Me to save him. What Peter didn't know was that he was already safe because he was focused on Me. The second he started focusing on the waves and the wind, he began to doubt. He took his focus off of Me, that's why he fell in."

Jesus stopped walking and looked at me. "Victor, never take your focus off of Me when things are not going your way. I am there in the middle of your storms."

We finally made it to the other side of the body of water. "This place is beautiful," I described.

"Only about seven to eight people on average come here daily after they die on earth," Jesus informed.

"How is that?" I asked. "There are so many churches out there. Pastors are out there preaching Your word."

Jesus began to walk. "The majority of My people are walking the wide path that leads to destruction with the non-believers," Jesus taught. "Many of the believers think it's just the non-believers who are on the wide path. In reality, many Christians are on the wide path with the unbelieving. Many of the believers in the church have not repented of their sins. They still live carnal lives outside of the church. Some of them are pastors, Victor. Luke 13:24 says to strive to enter at the straight gate. Non-believers don't strive to enter the straight gate ... for they are non-believers. I'm talking to the believers, Victor. Matthew 6:24 says you cannot serve two masters. You can't go to church serving My Father on Sunday, then serve Satan from Monday through Saturday. These are the lukewarm believers. I will spew out lukewarm believers because they are neither hot nor cold. The ones who are hot are the ones who are living a holy life. The ones who are cold are the non-believers. The ones who are lukewarm are the ones who are believers, but they still have not turned away from their sinful ways; instead, they hang on to their sinful ways while trying to live a holy life at the same time."

Jesus stopped walking and turned toward me. "Tell this to My church, Victor. They must know this. Many pastors have gone away from teaching, repenting, and striving to be holy. They think they can bring worldly ways into the church, and that dilutes the true gospel."

I closed my eyes and began to look at my past. I indulged in many things that were not of God. Lust, bitterness, drunkenness, and rebellion were just a few of the things I had in my heart at one time or another. I cussed, participated in lewd acts, and I told inappropriate jokes as well. Although I stayed away from these things since my encounter with Jesus, I felt deep down that if the opportunity presented itself, I would indulge in these sinful things again. I finally knew what I was to do! Jesus told me this while I was on my way to hell that night. Now I knew what it was I was supposed to do! It was to repent! I took a deep breath, turned toward Jesus, and I got on my knees.

"Lord Jesus, forgive me for the sins I committed against You. Thank You for taking my sins away. Sincerely, I repent, and I turn away from my sinful nature. Help me to move forward. Help me to walk the narrow and straight path to be more holy."

I began to cry at Jesus' feet. This cry came from deep within. I never cried like this before. It was a spiritual cry of repentance. Jesus lifted me up. "Your repentance is genuine, Victor."

Suddenly my garments began to glow even whiter! They were just as white as everybody I saw in heaven!

"You are now clothed in My righteousness," Jesus affirmed with a smile. He then put His hand on my shoulder.

"Go and tell My church what you have seen and what I have told you. I will be with you always."

I felt a confidence in me that was boiling inside me. The confidence was from everything that I learned over the past few months. Heaven was such a beautiful place. I wanted to stay here forever. The mere thought of me going back home saddened me.

"It's time to go back, Victor," Jesus directed. He held out His hand toward me. Reluctantly, I placed my hand in His, and instantly, we were in our meeting room. We both sat in our seats. "This will be the last time I visit you like this," Jesus stated.

I nodded my head. "I'm going to miss this," I shared. "I don't want this to end." Tears began to well up in my eyes.

Jesus smiled at me. "Why are you crying, My child?" He said. "I am always with you." He got up and wiped my tears away with His thumbs, yet they remained dry. "I have to collect these," He explained.

I gave Jesus a big hug. I held on to Him. I didn't want to let Him go. I cherished that moment as if it were my last. "I love You, Jesus," I revealed.

"I love you, too," Jesus reciprocated. "You are going to do great things for Me. Allen, Kyle, and Candace will do great things for Me, too."

"What about Vicky?" I asked.

"Your companion will do great works for Me as well,"

Jesus replied.

As soon as it registered in my mind what Jesus said, I was suddenly back in my body, and with a loud gasp, I was awake. I sat up in my bed. "Thank You for everything You have done for me, Jesus," I whispered.

I was still sad because I knew Jesus was not going to visit me in my dreams anymore. Nevertheless, I was comforted in knowing that I was going to see Him face to face again, I just didn't know when, and the next time I see Him, it will be permanent.

CHAPTER 21

FIVE YEARS LATER

****

Five years have passed since that final encounter with Jesus. To say a lot has changed for the better since then would be a huge understatement. Kyle and his wife, Candace, are now the lead pastors at our church. I always felt that they had the tools to become lead pastors someday. They were destined for that position, in my opinion.

Allen leads a small group every summer to do missionary work overseas. He is also the youth pastor at our church now. He's married and has twin boys. He continues to share his testimony about how God used me to save him from suicide and alcoholism that day.

My dad is now a member of our church. He

occasionally volunteers at many of our events. He's had to change and unlearn many things. It's been a tough road for him spiritually, and he is determined to finish the race. Our relationship has blossomed in a spiritual way since he gave his life to Jesus.

I proposed to Vicky one week after my final encounter with Jesus. There was no need to wait. She felt the same way, and she said yes. We got married a month later in a private ceremony at our church. It was nothing special to the eyes of the casual person. However, for Vicky and me, it was everything. We didn't even have rings yet. We both just wanted to show God that we were committed to each other with our hearts. My mother went into her attic and found Grandma Victoria's wedding ring. She had it restored and gave it to Vicky. Kyle and Candace chipped in with Allen and my dad, and they bought me a wedding band. God has truly blessed me with a loving family.

Vicky and I have a four-year-old daughter now. I travel from church to church as a guest speaker. I educate the church about the things Jesus showed me. I let them know that many of them are on that broad path, not just the non-believers. I show them many of the scriptures Jesus showed me that back me up. I've received many letters and emails from pastors who don't believe me. They call me a liar and a false teacher. It gets me down sometimes, but Vicky is always there to help me get through those tough times. I have received letters from pastors that told me they had examined their walks, and they are working to narrow their personal paths. This encourages me to press on and to continue the work Jesus has entrusted me with. It's up to me to spread the word to the church.

Because of my travel schedule, Kyle and Candace's ministry, and Allen's ministry and travel, we rarely have our round table talks like we used to. Sometimes, we all get on the phone and talk to each other to catch up.

I look back at my first encounter with Jesus. I was in such a condition that He actually had to show up in my dreams to get through to me. It took the love of a praying great-grandmother who died years before I was born, to erase years of the unbelief of Jesus in our family line. The days of unbelief in our family line stops here. Our house serves the Lord, and we will bring our child up in the ways of our Lord.

I know Jesus is still with me. I still think about our time together when I saw Him face to face. I actually walked with Him and talked with Him just as His disciples did over two thousand years ago. I really missed that period in my life. I can only imagine when He comes back how everything will be.

I'm so thankful for everything Jesus has done for me. Jesus really is everything to me. He's my best friend. I can't believe there was a time when I didn't believe in Him. My great-grandmother set things in motion for Jesus to search her descendants to find a believer, and He found me, a non-believer, and turned my life completely around.

So, there you have it. The story of how Jesus came to me in my dreams. A once in a lifetime encounter that I will cherish for the rest of my life. I was a "blind" non-believer who can now "see." I was deaf to hear the Word, now my ears are open to hearing it. I was a dead man who became born again.

It's not up to me to make you believe. I'm just a messenger. I chose to become His vessel to spread the word of God to His people. It's up to you, for you have free will to choose. I only ask one thing for everyone who reads this. Clear your mind and search your heart. Ask Jesus to reveal Himself to you. If you can honestly do that, then I can guarantee you Jesus will come to you. In Matthew 10:39, Jesus says, "He who finds his life will lose it, and he who loses his life for My sake will find it." I can honestly say that I have completely lost my life, and I have found something that will benefit me in this life and the next.

My name is Victor Storey. I am not perfect, but Jesus used me to be perfect in this moment to bring you the truthful testimony I now share with you. I pray you receive this as I have received it. May God bless you and your household.... amen.

ABOUT THE AUTHOR

****

A.R. Johnson is a U.S. Air Force veteran who, inspired by a dream that he had, began writing stories that would later become books. Like his character in the story, A.R. has had his own experience with Christ, which he has shared with hundreds of people at church and on social media. A.R. has a heart to see people blessed and free, and has also written a children's novel, soon to be published. He currently resides in Illinois with his beautiful wife and daughter.

9 780578 303611